ANDREI *and the* SNOW WALKER

In The Same Boat

ANDREI *and the* SNOW WALKER

LARRY WARWARUK

Editor for the Series, Barbara Sapergia.
Edited by Barbara Sapergia and Geoffrey Ursell.
Cover painting and interior illustrations by Susan Gardos.
Cover and book design by Duncan Campbell.
"In The Same Boat" logo designed by Tania Wolk, Magpie Design.
Printed and bound in Canada by Houghton Boston, Saskatoon.

National Library of Canada Cataloguing in Publication Data

Warwaruk, Larry, 1943-
Andrei and the snow walker

(In the same boat)
ISBN 1-55050-213-1

1. Ukrainian Canadians–Juvenile fiction. 2. Métis–Juvenile fiction. I. Title. II. Series.
PS8595.A786A82 2002 JC813'.54 C2002-910912-4
PZ7.W25822AN 2002

10 9 8 7 6 5 4 3 2 1

401-2206 Dewdney Ave
Regina, Saskatchewan
Canada S4R 1H3

available in the US from:
Fitzhenry and Whiteside
195 Allstate Parkway
Markham, Ontario
Canada L3R 4T8

The publisher gratefully acknowledges the financial assistance of the Saskatchewan Arts Board, the Canada Council for the Arts, including the Millennium Arts Fund, the Government of Canada through the Book Publishing Industry Development Program (BPIDP), and the City of Regina Arts Commission, for its publishing program.

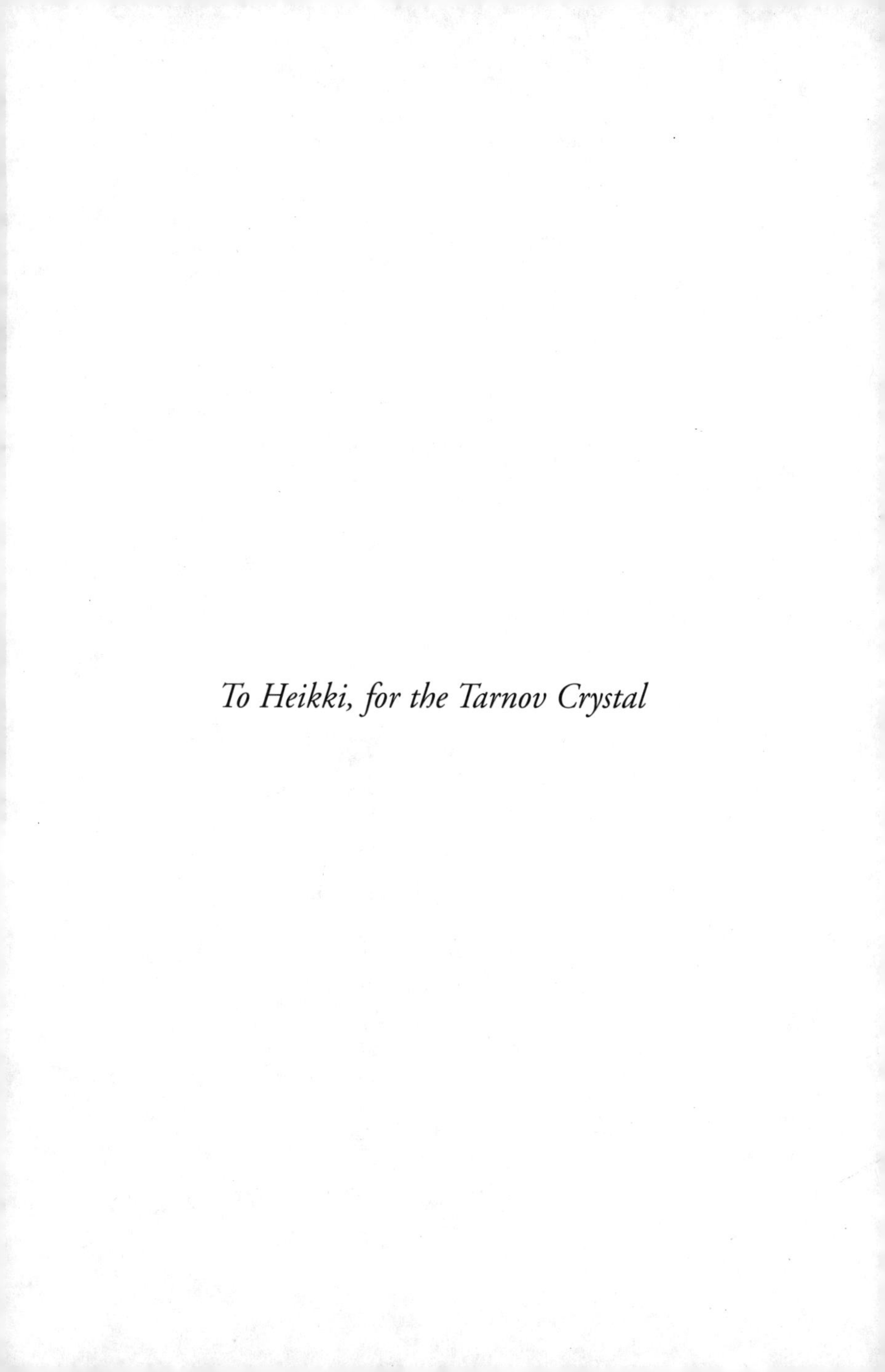

To Heikki, for the Tarnov Crystal

April 1900

CHAPTER 1

ANDREI SLIPS OUT OF BED BEFORE DAWN ON THE MORNING the Baydas are to leave for Canada. Without waking his parents, his sister, or his grandfather, he tiptoes out the door. Surely he's awake, yet everything around him is so still, the only sound a solitary chirp of a hidden bird, the only sight the shadow of village houses.

Today he's about to embark on a journey across the world. Last summer he steered a raft on the river behind their house, but that's nothing compared even to just the thought of crossing the ocean! It is the first day of April, 1900, and Andrei's family is leaving their home in the Ukrainian village of Zabokruky in Horodenka province.

It's in these final moments just before sunrise that he spots the light. Something is going on at the old graveyard, on one of the earthern mounds where Cossack warriors were buried three hundred years ago. Many times he has run up and down these hills. This morning as he leans against the willow fence, peering out at them, he notices a movement, the shadow of a man approaching a cross at the top. Then all at once the light flashes. Andrei rubs his eyes, then watches as it steadies into a golden halo circling the cross. At its centre throbs a red sparkle.

At first Andrei's only puzzled. But all of the sudden his left temple twitches. His eyesight blurs as if a fog surrounds him, and he loses any sense of where he is. Slowly the fog lifts; the halo around the cross reappears, rolls down the mound and then to the river. He's taken with it, transposed at once to walk along the river to where his grandfather has netted fish. He doesn't know how long he's been walking, or if he walks at all, or is he being carried? The dark water below him transforms into a road of gold bricks. The brush along its edges hangs heavy with branches full of coins of silver and gold. On a rolling plain beyond the river's far bank, a herd of riderless Cossack horses runs in spirals like the wind.

Andrei rubs his eyes again. The vision's disappeared and he's back at the yard. The halo has returned to the cross and then a black figure takes it. Andrei reaches as if to grab a handful of coins from a willow branch, but instead he grasps a stick from the willow fence. What really has he seen? Has he been anywhere? Should he wake his grandfather? Would anyone believe Andrei?

He squints at the sharp sparkle of the sun's rim on the horizon. He goes to the well and, pulling on the rope, he draws a pail of water and drinks. He wonders about the light. Was it a signal lighting his way to Canada? The gold a promise of fortune? Was it meant for him alone? Andrei sneaks back into the house and his bed. Maybe he can sleep for a little while yet.

AFTER AN HOUR HE RISES. Was it a dream, the shadowy time before dawn, when he had gone outside? When he had seen the strange light around the cross? The moments when the night was ending and the day not yet starting and Andrei couldn't be sure if he was awake or not. The river of gold? Had there really been a light, a golden halo and a red gleam, and had he really seen the fleeting shadow of a man? Had he really been outside and then gone back to sleep? Had he really left the yard? He thinks that he was awake, and now he hears the neighing of horses, and this time he's awake for sure.

The neighbour's wagon has come. He runs outside. Dido is standing in front of the horses, animals with coats as black as a Tartar's eyes. He's slicing a turnip. Andrei watches as his grandfather holds out his hand. He pats the horses' noses and rubs their ears.

"Have you ever owned a horse?" Andrei asks. Dido pulls at the withered skin of his neck, a turkey neck, the old man skin and bone.

"Before you were born, Andrei. Before the Polish *pahn* fleeced the very land from under our feet. And then I worked the *pahn's* horses. Groomed them, trimmed their hooves, hammered on shoes. A Cossack is not a Cossack without a horse. In Canada we will have no *pahn* landlord to rob us. In Canada I will buy a horse."

He feeds the last of the turnip, then walks down the road toward the church. "Don't leave without me," he says.

Three men from the village and Andrei's father, his tato, carry the trunk out of the house. They edge through the doorway, the two men at the front, hands gripped to the bottom of the trunk, struggling under the weight, stepping backwards with their heads turned to see their way, Tato telling them not to stumble. Neighbours gather to watch. Old ladies in a sea of white shawls, hands held as if in prayer, *Oi, oi, oi,* murmuring, wiping tears. Boys and girls jostling to see up close, waving to the waiting wagon, "Goodbye, Andrei, goodbye!" By himself, a neighbour boy Petrus Shumka, leans against the side of the house. He beckons to Andrei's sister Marusia.

Andrei's mother, Paraska, bows to kiss the door frame, hands held fast to the wood, wailing lamentations as she always did for others at funerals, though now weeping for herself, spilling her grief as if their leaving is death. Andrei follows his father into the house. Stefan Bayda stands, his fingers gripping his cap, pressed to his leg. He faces the wall, now empty of its Holy pictures. On this whitewashed wall, the yellowed squares where the pictures hung stare blindly like the eyes of ghosts. Tato turns, and jams the cap back on his head.

"Come on, Andrei. Why do you stand there? Do you think you have all day to gape at nothing?"

"Everybody on the wagon," Tato says. "Where is Dido?"

"At the church," Andrei's mother says as she arranges a place to sit in the centre of the wagon. "He must have gone to pray at Baba's grave."

"And Marusia. Where is Marusia?"

"Where do you think?"

"The Shumka boy? Does she think she can take him with us?"

"No, but she can say goodbye. It's all right for her to say goodbye. Don't you remember when you were young?"

"And foolish," Tato says. "Andrei, get your sister."

He runs to the back of the house and to the river, his dog Brovko trailing behind, whimpering. Brovko knows we are leaving, Andrei thinks. He stops, turns around and rubs the big dog's neck, his ears, his eyebrows...*brova*...the hair down over his eyes. That's his name, Brovko, Andrei's dog that looks like eyebrows. He runs in circles around Andrei. He wants to play, Andrei thinks, and he throws a stick into the river. The dog plunges into the water.

Marusia stands on the riverbank facing Petrus Shumka. She holds a branch of cherry blossoms. Neither says a thing while Petrus stares at her, and she gazes to the ground at her feet, tears forming in her eyes. She bends to set the blossoms on the rippling stream.

"Tato wants you," Andrei says.

Petrus kicks at the dirt. He's wearing his best clothes. Soft leather shoes with straps wound halfway to his knees. Red breeches, white linen shirt, embroidered vest, and a floppy hat with a sprig of the cherry blossoms in its band. He has just the start of a fuzzy moustache.

"Goodbye," he says to Marusia. "Write me a letter as soon as you can. Maybe some day I will come to Canada."

Brovko races up the bank, shaking and spraying water, stick gripped in his mouth.

"Get away with that shaking," Marusia says. Petrus steps back, laughing. He faces Andrei. "Don't worry. I will look after your dog."

Andrei, Marusia, Petrus, and then the dog straggle from behind the house toward the wagon, now surrounded by the villagers.

"Paraska," old lady Totchuk yells to Andrei's mother, "how can I write to you?"

"I will write when we are settled." Andrei knows his mother is proud to say this. For five years, as often as she could, she'd follow him to the reading hall, and she would stay a while to learn something herself. The village will miss her, and not only for reading and writing letters. She sings at weddings, and she cries at funerals.

The five Holochuk girls and Petrus's older sister Martha stand in a row, each waving an embroidered cloth to Marusia, cloths each of them hope will one day bind their husbands to them. Poor Martha. She had to raise her own brothers and sisters after her mother died. She's missed out on getting a husband, unless some old widower finds her.

Andrei thinks the youngest Holochuk, Natasha, is waving at him, her eyes blue, her hair the colour of wheat straw in sunlight. This year, would she have given him a specially decorated Easter egg if he wasn't leaving? He's too young to think about girls, but Natasha's pretty all the same. Tekla, the third oldest and the prettiest, runs over to Petrus. She winks at Marusia and holds on to Petrus's arm.

"I'll look after him," she says.

A neighbour, Olya Munchka, comes forward. "I never

told you before, Paraska. I didn't know how. But now I won't see you again." She breaks into a fit of sobs, wipes her face with the folds of her apron. "Last fall," she says, "I was the one who took cabbage from your garden. Please, can you forgive me?"

"You?" Paraska says. "I thought it was somebody's cow. She waves her hand and laughs. "It's all right, Olya. What can I do now with cabbage?"

Dido returns with the village priest. The people gather around. The priest leads them in prayer, then sprinkles Holy Water to each corner of the wagon. Tato nods and the driver snaps his whip above the horses' heads. The wagon jerks, its wheels rumbling in the slow movement out of the village toward the distant hillside of ancient Cossack battles, the direction of the mounds.

The valley fills with song. The people of the village follow the wagon, the melody of the Holochuks shrill in the air, deep male voices rumbling like the sound of cranes...*Croo, croo, croo,* like every spring and fall when the birds are moving across the sky. *Croo, croo, croo. Croo, croo, croo,* as if the sound shakes the hillsides. *Croo, croo, croo.* Petrus Shumka singing, *See my friend, the sky. See, the cranes on high. Wing to wing they fly together, fading as they fly.* His sister Martha, her song forlorn, its beauty in its sadness...*Croo, croo, croo. Though the wings are true. You may perish on the ocean, like some weary crew.* The wagon creaks and horses snort, adding to the sound.

"Brovko!" Andrei yells. Petrus rests on one knee, his arm around the dog's neck.

"Goodbye, Brovko."

The dog howls, lunging, Petrus holding him back.

"You'll get another dog," Dido says. "Forget Brovko. Petrus will look after him. Come on, cheer up." He pats Andrei on the back. "Have a good look back there behind the dog and all the people. You won't see the village ever again." Twelve-year-old Andrei has climbed up on the trunk. He wants a view to the front of the wagon so he can see where their adventure is taking them.

He sits with feet splayed, then pushes down with his arms, raising his body. Lifting one hand at a time, he swings his legs back and forth like an acrobat.

But his grandfather looks back, his hand shading his brow. "We see everything from here." He fingers his willow flute and plays a few merry notes, like an wizard casting a spell of blessing on the lands they are leaving. Andrei's grandfather...his dido, Danylo Skomar, in his heart a Cossack, bends from the waist, feet dangling, pointing to the scenery with his flute. "Remember these pictures, my boy. Some day you will be Dido, and you will tell your grandson about the very last things you saw leaving your homeland."

"Is it far to where we are going?"

"Far away, to some cowboy land." Dido Danylo swings his flute above his head, round and round as if it were a lariat. "Saskatchewan River."

"What is a cowboy?"

"A great horseman, just like a Cossack riding on the steppe, racing the wind across the plain."

Andrei feels as if he's flying through the air, a sky filled with a fragrance of cherry blossoms. He feels that he could ride a horse into the distance like a cowboy over endless plains.

"Careful you don't fall off. Sit here." Danylo Skomar strokes his hanging moustache. "Pay attention." The wagon courses along the road, the horses stepping high in a jolting rhythm almost as if hesitating. The village ever so slowly grows smaller...the willow fences, the whitewashed houses, the fruit trees, the onion dome of the church, the fields in the rolling hills and valleys, the river trailing down from the Carpathian mountains. *Croo, croo, croo,* the sounds of the villagers growing faint. *Croo, croo, croo.*

"We travel across the ocean," Dido says.

It's real. They are leaving. When Andrei's father, Stefan Bayda, had heard that he, a poor Ukrainian peasant, could buy a farm in Canada for ten dollars, how could he resist? All he had owned here was one acre and a half. All winter Mama and Tato argued.

"Why should I eat cabbage soup all my life?" Tato said.

But Mama was afraid. "What if a storm comes on the ocean? We will sink!"

"No more silly talk," Tato said. "We cross the ocean. In Canada we will live like landlords."

Andrei knows about the ocean. He was seven when the school opened in their village. He's seen the world on a map. He has seen the ocean and Canada, but he wants to hear his grandfather tell it.

Andrei and Dido sit side by side, backs against the trunk. It's huge. Andrei's tato constructed it, and all day yesterday his mother and sister Marusia packed it with their winter clothing, the sheepskins, woven blankets, and feather-filled bedcovers to line the bottom of the chest. Holy pictures lay between pillows. Bowls, dishes, cups, and wooden spoons inserted here and there. A frying pan. An iron ring stand for cooking over an open fire. Tools...two axes, a hatchet, two sickles, a scythe, a drawknife, two spades, three hammers, two hoes and a rake, two handsaws, the shorter stick and leathers of their flail, Dido's fishnet...all covered with a blanket.

On top of this Andrei's mother laid their dress clothes, held her beads a moment pressed to her cheeks, then rolled them into a cloth pouch and laid it in. On the bench against the wall, under the empty spaces left from the removal of the Holy pictures, other cloth packets lay in rows. Marusia handed them to her mother, little cloth bundles of seeds to be placed among the clothes...onions, garlic, horseradish, corn, marigolds, sweet william, dried herbs. She wrapped candles, a prayer book, a small jar of Holy Water. Tato gave her a parcel. It was a handful of black soil wrapped in cloth, taken from the wheat field. It was midnight when finally Mama covered everything with her embroidered linens and the lid was closed.

As they approach the burial mounds, Dido talks on and on.

"Canada is on the other side of the world. There we will wear gold watches, just like the landlords."

"Are there Cossacks in Canada, like cowboys?"

"Only cowboys," Dido says, "and Indians."

"At school our teacher told us about Indians."

"What does the teacher know about Indians? How would he know?"

"He has a picture book from America."

"And what does he say?" Dido shakes his head. His Cossack braid snakes across his shoulder. His shaved head appears as if it's glowing in the sunlight.

"He says they ride horses."

"Not like Cossacks." Dido fishes a trinket from his vest pocket, a clay pipe he keeps tied in a cloth pouch. It's Dido's Cossack pipe, handed down from many generations. The pipe is of glazed white clay. The design of a poppy flower is carved on each side of the bowl. Dido never uses this pipe; he smokes with a regular one made of wood. The clay pipe is more like a treasure to him, and he has promised it to Andrei. Dido takes it out of the pouch as he often does, rolls it around in his fingers for a moment or two, then puts it away.

"Yes, Andrei, a Cossack can ride at full gallop, swing himself down and snatch a silk kerchief from the ground with his teeth. We have the world's greatest horsemen. We were the first to tame the horse. Three thousand years ago, our Scythian warriors rode far and wide across the grasslands of Ukraine. They introduced horses to the world. Horsemanship is in our blood." He cups his hands, yelling to his son-in-law, "Stefan! Tell the driver to stop."

Dido crawls down off the wagon and walks up to the stonework staircase of a burial mound. He stops at each step and kneels, bowing his head to the ground over and over, repeating the sign of the cross, thumb and two fingers touching his head, chest, shoulder, and shoulder. He prays each time with his eyes glued to the cross at the top of the mound. On reaching the summit he kisses the cross, picks up a clump of earth and crumbles it on his bald head, crosses himself three more times, each with a bow, then descends from the mound.

Andrei knows the history of the mounds. At school the teacher told of the ancient battles against Turks and Poles. He told of the Hetman Bayda-Vyshnevetsky with 35,000 Cossacks fighting on this hillside three hundred years ago. Sacred graves. Mounds like the graves of their Scythian forebears. No one plows the land of the battlefield. Andrei has often asked if the Hetman was his ancestor. And Dido Danylo has often said, "Of course!"

"Are there still Cossacks?" Andrei asks his grandfather.

"A few."

"Should I pray for them too?"

"Maybe you should."

"Where do they live?"

Andrei has asked these questions before. Dido never can say enough about Cossacks. How many times has he told the story of the Hetman Bayda-Vyshnevetsky? How many times has Andrei heard about the famous Cossack island fortress, the Seech, far to the east on the Dnipro River, and how the Hetman Bayda had started this brotherhood of Cossacks.

"Do they still live at the Seech?"

"No more," Dido says. "Maybe some day again."

"Who lives on the island now?"

"Farmers," Dido says. "The Empress Catherine brought them from far away to plow up the Ukrainian Steppes."

"Can farmers be Cossacks?"

"You should ask instead, can Cossacks be farmers? Could they have even wanted to be farmers when they could ride their horses across the steppes?"

Dido plays notes on his flute, then he sings a part of one of the many verses from the song of the Hetman Bayda. He doesn't sing the verses that he usually does, the ones with the Hetman riding a horse, or shooting arrows at an enemy from the Empire of the Turks. Instead he sings as the Ukrainian women do at weddings, calling for the Cossack to quit his roaming, his fighting, his drinking, and return to his family. Dido must be feeling sad that the Bayda family is leaving their homeland forever and will not be coming back:

Go home and quit your wandering life
You've children and a lovely wife...

Dido sings on and on, and he hums. Not long after the wagon pulls away from the burial mound, from over a ridge on the hillside, as if out of nowhere an old man appears. He's dressed in dirty grey sackcloth, his hair and beard straggling to his waist. He drags a cross hoisted on his shoulder, an assortment of stars and crescent moons carved into the wood. His eyes like cold crystal fix trance-like on Dido Danylo. Andrei remembers the moving shadow of early morning, the figure on the hillside just before the brilliant light appeared.

"Skomar!" In a hoarse whisper the old man repeats the family name of Andrei's Dido. "Skomar! Skomar!" as if in death's last gasps. He points at Dido. "I am your Uncle Skomar, and my time ends." He stands behind the wagon thirty feet from Andrei, the mounds far in the background. He shakes his finger, then gestures for Dido to follow him. The Holy man Skomar and Andrei's grandfather climb up the hill and disappear over the ridge.

The wagon driver and Andrei's father say nothing. Mama has often said that you must never interfere with fools or Holy men. Mystics have wandered the land for centuries, and God blesses those who respect these Holy fools.

They wait a long time. Finally Tato shouts to Andrei. "Go get him! Does he think we have all day?"

Andrei's familiar with the terrain, and even when he gets to the river, there should be nothing to upset his bearings. He's positive there isn't a spot anywhere along the river that he hasn't previously explored...unless away further upstream into the mountains where the Hutsul people live. But Dido and the Holy man can't have gone that far. All at once he feels again the strange sensations of the early morning. As he steps down a path through the shrubs to the river's bank, the twitch in his temple returns, like a seizure. In Andrei's vision the willow branches are laden again with coins and the river water's turned to a broad path of gold. A fog rises swirling in circles, and like Aladdin, Andrei's standing at the mouth of a cave. An energy like that of the morning draws him inside.

Through a fog of incense and rainbow colours, two Scythian warriors stand guard, each with sword, shield, and gold helmet, each with a horse at his side; a white horse and a red horse. For a moment Andrei sees the warriors as Dido and the Holy man, but each much younger. Then he recognizes himself on each face, himself a Scythian soldier, the earliest of Ukrainians. A halo glimmers on a flat stone altar, a red gleam at its centre.

The rainbow fog thickens and Andrei's lifted, swirling

round and round in its colours, until everything turns black. He remembers nothing more, only the vision in the cave, nothing more until he's back at the wagon with his grandfather. Dido carries a goatskin bag with something bulky inside.

"What do you have?" Tato asks.

For a moment it appears as if Dido's eyes are those of a madman. He stares back to the hillside.

"He is my uncle," Dido says. "He is of our Skomar family that goes back to the ancients."

"It's true?" Tato asks. "The Holy one is your uncle?"

"Skomar of the Scythians," Dido says, as if locked in a trance.

"What's in the bag?" Tato asks again.

"A relic of the Scythians," Dido says. Slowly the spell washes from his eyes. He rubs his hand twice across his chin as if brushing away a fly. "Maybe just from Gypsies."

"Scythians? Gypsies? What have you got to do with Gypsies? Is this some kind of treasure? Magic?"

Scythia, Andrei thinks. The sight in the cave stays with him. Overwhelms him. Dido has told him that the making of burial mounds began with the Scythians. No one knows where the Scythians came from or where they went. Only that they were warriors and that they lived before Cossacks. What does Dido have in the bag? Is it the golden halo?

"What is it?" Tato repeats.

"Ah, it's nothing," says Dido. "Just a bag. What can be more homely than goatskin?" And then he laughs.

"Something is funny?"

Dido pauses for a long moment, all the while tugging at

his moustache. "I'll tell you," he says, biting his lips. "Uncle told me that two hundred years ago a Skomar ran off with a woman. In Bukovyna...some Romanian girl. A Gypsy for all that, the fool said." He holds up the bag. "Her people had carried this with them for centuries."

"Scythians," Andrei blurts, as if he's taken up Dido's trance.

Dido turns his attention to Andrei, grabbing him by the shoulders and shaking him.

"There is Skomar blood in you also," Dido says. "You must hear. My Uncle Skomar said that there is a talisman in this bag that came from somewhere deep inside a Scythian burial mound. Robbed from the grave. He said it is a talisman that will reveal messages for lives yet unborn who will struggle far off in a new land."

"Take the bag away," Mama says. "Leave devil worship alone." She makes the sign of the cross three times across her breast. "Better yet to bury it in a pile of pig manure." She draws her shawl tightly over her shoulders.

"So," Tato says as he rubs his moustache with his fingers. Then he turns his attention to Dido. "Let's have a look in the bag."

Both Dido's hands clutch it to his lap. His eyes dart in all directions, and then he reaches for his own packing crate, opens it, and stuffs the bag under a bundle of clothing.

"I'm not to show a soul."

Dido waves his hand for the driver to get going. "Aren't we a fine bunch," he says. "Here we sit gabbing as if the train is supposed to wait for us."

Andrei tries to make sense out of what's happening. The halo was guarded by the ghosts of Scythian warriors. It has a power, and it is possible that the power's been assigned to Andrei himself, and it might give him the strength of a Scythian warrior. Andrei and Dido will carry the secret of this magic with them to their new place in Canada.

THEY TRAVEL TWELVE MILES to a siding on the railway to Lviv. From that city Dido says they will travel on a train across Europe all the way to Hamburg in Germany. There they will get on a ship.

They wait half an hour at the siding for the train to come. Three families from another village are waiting with them. Finally Andrei hears the train's whistle, hears the chug of its engine, and sees the belching smoke, a grey passenger car, and a red-painted wooden car behind it. The chugs come farther and farther apart as the engine slows, and steam shoots down from somewhere under its black steel belly, down between the rails of the cinder track. Andrei smells coal fire.

Men lift the trunk off the wagon and carry it to the open door of the freight car. Tato and Dido help cart belongings off the other wagons. The men talk about how there has been little rain in Horodenka province this spring and the crops will likely be poor. Tato gives their tickets to a man standing at the passenger car doorway, and Andrei follows Dido, Mama, and Marusia up the steel steps into the train.

CHAPTER 2

THE DOCKS IN HAMBURG ARE A CONFUSION OF SOUNDS, sights, and smells. Crowds of people talk in a variety of languages. Some shout and others laugh. Someone sells loaves of bread. Someone else, sausages. A man wearing a black floppy-brimmed hat plays polka music on a button accordion. The great ship blows its horn, sounding echoes across the bay. Seagulls swoop, screaming as they dive. The air smells of fish and salt brine. Mama clings to her own bag of bread and sausages as the family crams together up the ramp, following the throngs of passengers boarding the big ship, anxious to set out across the sea to Canada.

Andrei waits until they are well out to sea, below deck preparing for the night's sleep, before he asks Dido about the cave. They sit on Dido's crate, crouched under a metal staircase in the ship's hold.

"What cave?" Dido asks.

"Two Scythian warriors? A white horse and a red horse?"

"You talk nonsense."

"Then what did you see?"

"You should know. You came to get me on the riverbank. Old Uncle told me he was dying." Dido puffs on his pipe, and then for a second time he draws the smoke deeply into his lungs. As he continues speaking, the smoke releases. "He said he'd been caring for the relic many years in a Cossack cave far to the east, an ancient Scythian cavern in the bank of the Dnipro River."

"You weren't in a cave?"

"There are no caves along our river. Uncle pulled the bag from out of a bush and handed it to me. Told me to guard it with my life. That's just when you came to get me. 'Tato wants you to hurry,' you said."

"You didn't see a light?"

"Nothing."

"Did the Holy one speak of a power?"

"A Holy man trusts in the power of God."

Andrei shivers, though he's not cold. The damp air reeks with the smell of many people crowded together, their sweat and vomit, but none of this makes him shiver. Nor the smell of cattle manure. Dido says that people are shipped one direction, and the cowboys in Canada ship cattle back. People one way, cows the other. But it's not the living quarters for the ocean crossing that make Andrei shiver. It's his wonder about the talisman.

"Can I see it, Dido?"

"No," Dido says. "I'm to guard it. Carry it to Canada. Only there will it reveal its wants to us."

The next morning up on deck, Andrei's parents argue, their voices hushed. Mama insists they get rid of the goatskin bag as soon as they get to Canada. She wants nothing to do with what she calls Gypsy black magic. She says that if the authorities find out they are carrying the Devil, they won't let the family into the country. Tato says not to be so foolish. The Holy man is no Gypsy; he is a mysterious man of God. Why don't they simply wait to see what the bag contains? He thinks it's all nonsense anyway. Marusia pays no attention to them, lost as she is in her own world of memories. Dido says to argue about something else. Andrei wishes he could sneak below and search Dido's belongings, because his grandfather for sure won't show him. Dido thinks it's his mission alone, that Andrei's too young for such a responsibility. Little does Dido know what Andrei saw in the cave.

But Andrei realizes that he shouldn't dwell on his visions. There's a lot of other things on the ship to catch his attention. It's bigger than anything he could ever have imagined. Even the boat pulling them out of the Hamburg harbour was huge, but the ship *Carpathia* is as big as the mountains themselves. And it seems that the farther they sail away from land, when they can no longer see land, the boat seems small.

Seven days after Dido and Andrei talk about the talisman, the waves rise high, nothing is rooted, only railings and tables, and their bunks. All day and all night the ship bobs up and down like a duck, and the hundreds of people deep in the hold moan and groan and heave their suppers.

"Be brave," says Dido, hanging on to the staircase railing, peering upwards to the closed hatch above his head, appearing as if he is helmsman. "At Hamburg the officer said two weeks and the ship arrives at Halifax Port." Dido takes a crumpled paper from his pocket and marks off the strokes with a pencil. "Fifteen days," he says. "That is more than two weeks."

Marusia lies in her bunk, a cloth held to her mouth. Andrei's mother prays on her knees while his father sits on the edge of his bunk, his hands at his head, staring at the floor. Andrei stands on the floor, legs apart, fighting to keep his balance with the rocking of the boat.

"There's no need to be afraid," Dido says, counting the pencil strokes once again. "We should have arrived yesterday. Canada can't be far from here."

When morning comes and the storm subsides, they venture to the open deck and a blue sky. Someone has heard from the Captain himself that they will reach Halifax by nightfall. They'll be in Canada.

They arrive in a fog. The ship's horn blares into the darkness. Lights show through, faint beacons surrounding the arc of the harbour. A tugboat chugs far below in the dark, pulling the ship toward dock. Andrei had expected to be shouting the excitement of reaching land, but in the fog and darkness, he feels instead a lull, almost a dread of venturing into the unknown.

By midnight they are on another train, all through the night hearing the *click-click, click-click.* The car sways back and forth. Over and over the wheels click where the rails join, *click-click, click-click.* All the next day they wind through forests and rocks, by lakes, *click-click, click-click.*

Mama still carries her sack of bread and sausage. As each day passes, she doles out less and less. Will they ride this train forever? Andrei drinks water from a little paper cup. He leaves his seat time and again, parading to the water cooler. In a tiny room he presses a lever on the toilet. A flap opens and he sees the rush of the railbed passing underneath. Hears the *click-click, click-click.*

They reach Winnipeg, the place they've been told is their destination. Stay overnight in the immigration hall. Where are the farms everyone is supposed to go to? Can they walk to them from here? Tato talks to others, and he learns that they must go back again on the train.

Click-click, click-click. They are being sent further. Will they ever stop riding on trains? It seems like ages ago, the morning they left their village in the wagon, ages ago on the road where Brovko lurched and howled in the clutch of Petrus's arms. Andrei's dog is so far away he may as well be on the moon.

As much geography as Andrei learned in school, he really didn't know anything until now. Yet still he can't believe how big the world is.

CHAPTER 3

THEY SPEND THE NEXT DAY AT THE IMMIGRATION HALL, and at night, they board a train again. Early the next morning, at Regina, they change trains. Mama worries that their trunk will be lost and then what would they do? Tato says not to worry. The Canadian Pacific Railway knows what it's doing. The Baydas aren't the first family it's brought across the country.

Tato talks with others and learns that they go north now. In Saskatoon he's to go to the Land Office and get the paper for his farm. Ukrainian people are settling north of Saskatoon, on the east side of the Saskatchewan River. The paper will give Andrei's father title to one hundred times the amount of land he owned in Zabokruky, and all they want for it is ten Canadian dollars. He will have even a few dollars left to rent a wagon to take them to the homestead. At least he hopes he will have enough money left.

North of Saskatoon, at the railway station in Rosthern, the family reaches the final stages of its journey. The only travel left will be with horse and wagon. A light drizzle falls. The smells of fresh-cut clean white lumber waft from the many stacks piled on the platform. Andrei stands against the station wall with Marusia and his mother where Tato and Dido have left them while they go to hire a wagon. Families mill about all over. The freight carts are piled with steamer trunks, rolls of barbed wire, bags of flour, boxes of apples. Men shovel coal out of boxcars, and unload steel plows in wooden crates. Andrei runs up close to a boxcar ramp. A pair of horses step down, ears flat and nostrils flaring, jerking their heads, a handler pulling on the lines, coaxing the animals down.

"Out of the way!" the man says, and with his free arm he shoves Andrei to the side. His mother grabs his hand, pulling him back to the station wall.

All around him Andrei sees beds, cupboards, a steam-engine on a flatcar, crates of live chickens, and pigs. There is not a quiet spot anywhere. Empty wagons back up to the loading platform, the drivers tugging leather reins getting the horses to step back.

Andrei notices his father and Dido across the road. When his mother's turned the other way, he runs to join them on the sidewalk.

"Paraska said flour, for certain." Tato dumps coins from a cloth pouch into his palm, counting them; three of the bigger ones that are quarter dollars, and one ten-cent piece. After giving money to the wagon driver, they have less than one dollar left.

"And sugar," Dido says. "Tea." He gestures with open hands forward, palms up.

"The homestead's supposed to be in the bush," Tato says. "We can snare rabbits. Surely there must be rabbits."

"If that's all the money we have left," Dido says, "that little you have in your hand, we will have to make soup with Paraska's seeds."

"She said flour. Paraska has nothing left in the food bag. Only crumbs. You might be right. We might have to eat the seeds."

"You shouldn't have paid the wagon driver," Dido says.

"You are going to carry the trunk on your back? Twenty-five miles?"

Andrei follows them into a store. His father approaches the counter with his head lowered, staring at his coins. Dido nudges him with his elbow. Before either one says anything, the storekeeper behind the counter pats his white apron and shouts, "Well for goodness sake! Look who's come to Canada! If it isn't Stefan Bayda! And he brought old Danylo with him!"

Tato backs into Andrei, nearly knocking him to the floor. "I don't believe it!" he says.

Andrei recognizes him. The old storeman from Zabokruky. The Jewish merchant who sold his tavern to his nephew two years ago.

"You're here?" Tato says, spreading his hands apart then clapping them together. His coins fall to the floor and he bends to pick them up.

"As far as I know," Sam Zitchka says. "How's my store? Does my lazy nephew know what he's doing? Is he making any money?" Sam Zitchka laughs and hurries from behind the counter. He embraces Tato, kissing him on both cheeks, then repeating the ritual with Dido.

"You bought a farm?" he asks. "How are you getting there?"

Tato points out the window to the team and wagon. An elderly man smoking a pipe and wearing a wide flat-brimmed hat sits perched up front. His left arm appears to hang limp.

"Moise Desjardin. The ferryman," Zitchka says. "He's got only one good arm, but you can depend on him. Let me see your deed." Tato shows him the document he got from the Land Titles Office in Saskatoon. The merchant studies it a moment, then goes outside to the driver. Sam points at the paper and the driver purses his lips, puffs a few times on his pipe, then nods his head. Sam nods also and comes back into the store.

"You'll need some things," he says.

"I have money," Tato says, laying the coins on the counter one at a time. "But not a lot. It has been a long trip from our village."

"Maybe enough for tobacco," the merchant says. "But your credit is good here. If I can't trust a fellow countryman, who can I trust?"

In no time the counter's piled with a bag of flour, a smaller bag of cornmeal, a pail of lard, salt, tea, matches, a small pane of glass, a pound of iron nails. Zitchka writes the items down in a book.

"You're not asking me what I need?" Tato asks. "My wife has a long list in her head."

"Don't worry. I know what you need. You tell me if I miss anything."

"I can't pay till my first crop. Will there be season long enough this year?"

"Only God knows. But you and Danylo come back here as soon as you can. The Mennonites hire men to work on their farms. They pay you, and you pay me. Try Jake Klassen, just west of town."

"Thank you," Tato says. He shakes Zitchka's hand, and then he takes a step back and bows. "Thank you, thank you," he says again. He rubs the knuckles from both of his hands over his eyes, then moves forward to the counter and lifts the bag of flour to his shoulder. Dido, Andrei, and the merchant carry the remaining supplies to the wagon.

Mama stands at the edge of the railway platform, a hand on each cheek. *"Oi!"* she says. "*Oi! Oi!"* She stares at the load of groceries, then turns to Marusia. "*Oi! Oi! Oi!* See, Marusia? See what they have?" But at the very next moment she faces Tato again, and her look of joy and amazement changes to a frown of doubt and suspicion.

"I can't believe it either," Tato says. "Remember Sam Zitchka?" Mama nods. "He's the storekeeper here."

"What are you telling me?" Mama asks. "Sam Zitchka. On the other side of the world, and here is Sam Zitchka. And you didn't steal those groceries."

"Honest to God, he was there in the store, and he offered to help us."

"Not only *offered,*" Dido says. "He insisted."

"That's right," Tato says. "'Pay me in November,' Zitchka said. 'After the harvest.' He gave me the flour just like that, and corn meal, salt, matches, even a glass for a window, and a pound of iron nails. He said that there is a Mennonite farmer, Klassen, close by here who needs hands to work on his farm as soon as Dido and I can get back. We will come to earn money as soon as we get you settled at the homestead."

"Where is this home?" Mama asks, with a hint of joy on her face.

"Moise Desjardin will take us part way," Tato says. "To the river. His nephew will take us from there." Moise sits up on the wagon, his only movement a slow motion of his right hand holding a pipe, a blow of smoke; and then with the pipestem clenched in his teeth, he raises his hand and tugs gently on the broad and stiff brim of his black hat.

"At the river we cross on a ferry," Tato says. "Sam Zitchka told me that this old man's nephew is running the ferry for him while he came here for mail. Zitchka says that this nephew has even better horses that can take us to the homestead."

The Baydas leave Rosthern, heading east through drizzle toward the Saskatchewan River. So far the land is flat as the land of Cossacks on the Steppe, all of it grassland patched with dull grey bluffs of leafless poplar. The air is filled with the sweet smell of the grass. They had been warned about biting flies and mosquitoes, but strangely there are none. Maybe it's too early in the season. Andrei and Dido sit up on the trunk, facing to the front. They will come to a broad valley. At the station Father was told for the second time that the land where Ukrainians are settling lies on the other side of this valley's river.

The driver reaches over with his right arm and pulls the lever for the wheel brakes, the wagon skidding down into the valley, leather breeching strained in the white-foamed sweat on the rumps of the horses. One of the horses is limping.

The trail winds through patches of brush, the river wandering far below, visible now and again, a broad river with stretches of exposed sand. Andrei can see the hills on the other side, like the Carpathians, but not as green, the trees not yet in leaf, the new grass just beginning.

"See the hills, Dido?"

"Not really hills," Dido says, lifting his smoldering pipe and pointing to each side of the wagon. "Here a river has cut a broad valley. See far across to the other side? More than a mile, I'm guessing. Our trail winds far below us to the water, but this valley must at one time have been filled with a very big river."

At the riverbank they wait for the ferry. As it nears, Andrei watches the cable stretched across the river, sees it taut on the boat's turning pulleys, the river's current propelling the boat. Moise's nephew, who Sam Zitchka talked about, lifts a rope from a post and lowers the ferry's apron to the shallow water at the shore. The horses walk into the water, skittish, the way the Holochuk girls would wade into the river at Zabokruky, and the animals step up in a hurry onto the ramp, without Moise's urging. Andrei hears the knocks and thuds and clacks of their hooves striking the plank decking. He considers that two, and no more than three wagons could fit on this ferry. That's all there is, an open deck with square wooden posts supporting a waist-high railing along each side.

The nephew wears a black hat with a high crown and a wide, flat brim. He has the same dark skin as Moise, though he's much younger, reminding Andrei of Petrus Shumka. He has a sash tied around his waist like a Ukrainian. He talks to Moise in a language different from that spoken by the officials on the train.

Moise points to the Baydas. The nephew shrugs then nods his head. Andrei watches as he turns a wheel that pulls on the cable, somehow swinging the bow to face upstream, and the boat starts its journey back across the river.

In less than ten minutes, they are at the other side. The nephew drives Moise's team onto the east shore and up the bank to a barnyard. A boy the size of Andrei sits on a rail. Two black horses look out over the same rail. When the wagon comes to a stop, Mama peers up to the boy and then to the young man.

"What people are you?" Mama asks.

"I am Métis," the nephew says in broken Ukrainian. "I am Gabriel Desjarlais. Métis like my Uncle Moise." He steps off the wagon and unhitches the team. "We'll use my horses. Uncle Moise's mare has a limp. Uncle Moise wasn't born yesterday. He has your three dollars, and I take you. Your names are...?"

"I am Andrei, and this is Marusia," Andrei says.

"Marusia," Gabriel says, doffing his hat to Andrei's sister. "That is *Marie*, in the French language, and my brother here, his name is Chi Pete."

"Shouldn't your uncle take us the rest of the way?" Mama asks. She whispers to Tato, and Andrei attempts to hear what she's saying. Something about Gypsies. Now and then a band of Gypsies used to camp by their village. Mama was always telling Andrei to stay away, even if she herself would visit one of their women to have her fortune told. She's whispering to Tato, wondering if these dark-skinned men at the ferry are Gypsies.

"Ahh," Tato says, "What do you women think, Paraska? Just because they aren't Ukrainian, you think they will cheat you? Did the Jewish merchant cheat us?"

"You must be Indians," Dido says. "I heard our countrymen at the station talk of battles up and down these riverbanks. The Indians crippled a steamship."

"The Métis," Gabriel says. "Louis Riel. Gabriel Dumont. Uncle Moise fought with them. He fought three days defending Batoche and had a bullet go through his upper arm." Gabriel talks while he and his young brother hitch the fresh team to the wagon. Soon they are back on a trail heading east through country more rugged, more heavy with bush than the land they had already covered west of the river.

Dido has chosen to sit up at the front where he can talk with Gabriel.

"Your uncle doesn't speak Ukrainian?" Dido asks.

"No, just French, Cree, and English."

"He fought in a battle? Why were they fighting?"

"For the freedom of our Métis people," Gabriel says. "For our land."

"You lost?" Dido asks.

"Our riflemen ran out of bullets," Gabriel says. "Uncle Moise could tell you more if he knew your language."

"Our Cossacks fought to save our land," Dido says. "Three hundred years ago. Hetman Bayda-Vyshnevetsky with thirty-five thousand Cossacks riding on horses and swiping with sabres that could cut a man in half."

"They lost?" Gabriel asks.

"Not at Zabokruky. They successfully defended our village from the Polish army."

"And three hundred years later, where is Ukraine?" Tato asks. "The Austrian kings rule Zabokruky, and the Polish landlords own the land."

"Thirty-five thousand Cossacks," Dido says, as if refusing to hear what Tato has said.

"You are French?" Tato asks. "Sam Zitchka told me that your uncle speaks French, and a Native language...some kind of Indian. Anyway, your uncle is supposed to know where to take us. Zitchka assured me that your uncle knows. But what do you know?"

"You have the paper," Gabriel says. "I can find the iron stake."

It's a strange country, all new to Andrei's father. He passes the deed to Gabriel and shrugs his shoulders. "What else can a man do?" he says, turning to Mama. "Paraska, it is lucky that here in Canada we found Sam Zitchka. He knows who we can trust."

"Only four more miles," Gabriel says. Andrei likes the young man's looks, especially the hat. Even Marusia sneaks a glance at him. Andrei decides that the Baydas will do just fine. Everything will be all right. Besides, there is still the Skomar talisman inside the bag to think about.

Chi Pete sits at the front of the wagon with Gabriel. Andrei wishes that he could be there too. The boy turns his head now and then, glancing back with eyes half-closed.

Across the river and out of the valley, they follow a trail through a countryside filled with bush, meadow, water, and hills. Ducks swim, young ones trailing in lines after their mothers. The drizzle of rain has stopped, but the sky remains heavy with clouds. Mama peers around in every direction, eyes cautious, ever so watchful. Nobody lives out here. Where are they going to sleep? What if it starts raining again? She turns to Tato. He remains stone-faced, staring out at the wall of trees.

Andrei wonders if the boy Chi Pete has a horse of his own. If he hunts. If he has a rifle.

"Eggs," Mama says, pointing as a duck flies up from its nest. "Are they good to eat?"

The wagon stops. "You boys jump off and gather them," Gabriel says. "We can have eggs for supper."

By late afternoon the party has found the survey stake and the homestead quarter, matching the numbers to those on Tato's paper: sw 8/42/28/w3.

"Here we are," Gabriel says. Andrei gazes all around. There is no village, no house anywhere, just trees and grass, and it's starting to rain again. They are in a small clearing, just big enough for a house and yard, and in the distance they see what looks like a tiny lake, which Gabriel says is a slough. He points west in the direction they have come.

"There are fish in the river," he says.

"Lots of wood here to keep us warm," Tato says.

"Lots of wood to keep out the sun," Mama says, looking up at rolling clouds of black and blue.

"Lots of wood for a good house," Tato says.

Everyone gets off the wagon. Gabriel and Chi Pete unhitch the horses and tether them out to graze. The family stands motionless in a circle, facing one another as if uncertain what to do next.

Finally Tato climbs back up on the wagon and takes a shovel from the trunk. He digs into the sod, turning over heavy clumps. Both he and Dido scoop lumps of black dirt with their hands, crumbling it and letting the soil fall through their fingers. Mama joins them. She cups the soil in her hands, smelling it. They eye each other, and Tato nods. On their knees, the three adults make the sign of the cross. Mama motions for Marusia and Andrei to join them. Off by the horses, both Gabriel and Chi Pete do the same.

After the prayer, Andrei's father opens the trunk again, taking out an axe and hatchet, and the iron ring stand to place over a cooking fire. If Andrei can chop some dry firewood, Mama can fry duck eggs. They've bought flour, lard, and salt at the store, and mushrooms grow everywhere in the bush.

Chi Pete says something in their own language to his older brother.

"Why not?" Gabriel says, taking up the hatchet. He cuts a willow ten feet long, peels bark in long strips to fashion a loop snare, and binds it tightly to the end of the pole. "If you wish, follow me," he says, and he leads the curious party into the bush.

Gabriel puts his finger to his lips, then points upward to a tree. Chi Pete puts his hand on Andrei's shoulder. No one should move an inch. A bird sits on a branch. Gabriel lifts the pole, placing the loop around the bird's head, and with a jerk he has the bird held fast in the snare.

Back at their village, Andrei has many times watched his mother pluck the feathers off a chicken. But Gabriel doesn't do this. What he does is so quick and easy that Andrei can't tell for sure how it happens. Gabriel sets the bird down on its back, spreads its wings and steps on them. In one motion, a quick jerk, he pulls on the claw feet, and like magic, the bird's dressed, or undressed. It's as if Gabriel has unwrapped a parcel. He's pulled away the feathers and skin, taking with it the bird's head, the backbone, and the insides. He breaks off the wingtips and hands the remaining meat to Tato.

"Will you and your brother be so kind then to join us for supper?" Tato asks with a big grin on his face.

"We will be honoured to," Gabriel says.

Tato hands the skinned bird to Mama, then turns around in a full circle, all the while looking up over the tops of the trees. "All of this, ours," he says and he spreads his hands wide. Mama and Dido peer into the trees. Marusia reaches into the chest and pulls out the cast iron frying pan.

Mama browns the meat in the frying pan, and then she stews it with wild mushrooms and dumplings made with the flour. She fries the duck eggs. Then she takes more flour and makes a fried bread. Marusia gets dishes and eating utensils from the trunk, fills plates, and hands the food around. Andrei is ever so hungry, and he could swear that he has never in his life tasted anything as good as this. He's never felt as relaxed...certainly not since he has left his home in Zabokruky. He wishes only that he could feed a morsel of his fried bread to Brovko. His dog would like it, especially with the gravy. He can see that his two new friends like it.

"It looks and tastes like my mother's bannock," Gabriel says, as he sops gravy from his plate with the bread.

They sip hot tea and for a long time stare at the fire, until Marusia starts gathering up dishes. Tato shakes Gabriel's hand. Andrei shakes Gabriel's hand too, and then Chi Pete's.

As the Métis brothers drive off in their wagon, Gabriel waves to Marusia washing the dishes at the slough. She stands still a moment, her fingers gripped to her apron in folds, but one hand releases, and she waves back. Andrei wonders if he'll see Chi Pete and Gabriel ever again. Now the family is on its own completely, and they have no idea where they are. Soon it will be dark, and who knows what might be out there in the bush? All they have are the belongings they hauled off the wagon and set on the bare ground.

Where can they sleep? The sky is now even more blue-black, from the clouds thickening and the coming of night. They don't even have a wagon to crawl under.

"Under that tree," Tato says. "Bring the provisions before the flour gets wet." At the southern end of their small meadow, forty feet away at the forest edge, stands a tall spruce tree. "Help with the trunk." The family carries it to the tree. The trunk might help to block any wind sweeping in rain from the northwest. Mama digs through the trunk, retrieving feather-filled bed coverings, woven blankets, and sheepskins. All night they lie under the spruce boughs, trying to sleep, and trying to keep out the damp.

IN THE MORNING they start to build something that will shelter them better than living like a den of foxes. They start on their *buda.* Dido likes to think he's an expert when it comes to building a *buda.* Cossacks used to build *budas* on their island fortress. They built them in the field, mostly out of willows, mud, and grass. A Scythian warrior lived in a *buda.* But here with all this forest they can build one very solid, and build it quickly; there will be nothing to it.

While the men chop trees, Andrei trims off branches. Mama and Marusia try to gather grass dry enough to spread under the spruce. They will have a night or two yet to spend under there, and nobody got much sleep last night. Tato tells Andrei to dig two holes, one for each of the two main upright posts. They are to be twenty feet apart.

Tato sets a post in the first hole. "Perfect," he says. He has chosen a poplar with a fork eight feet up its trunk. He sinks the post in the hole two feet deep, and tamps clay and stones around the base. Dido has another post identical to Tato's, and he waits for Andrei to finish the second hole.

But it's not as simple to build a *buda* as Dido said. Not in the rain. Mama and Marusia can't find grass dry enough to spread under the spruce. They can't even find anything dry enough to make a fire. They have to somehow keep the flour, cornmeal, and sugar dry. Last night they put the provisions under the spruce with them and covered everything with sheepskins. And now by mid-morning everybody's hungry, and they have no fire to cook things on. Mama can't even fry pancakes.

"Let's keep working," Tato says. "Maybe the sun will

come out."

Dido and Tato lift a long log onto the forks of the two main posts. Under this beam, it's Andrei's job the rest of the day to dig an excavation. The floor of their *buda* is to be a foot and a half below ground level and five feet wide. He's to leave an additional three feet all along one side to serve as a bench, and a place where everyone can sleep.

By noon the sun is out, and with Dido's help at whittling wood shavings from a dead tree branch, Mama finally has a fire going. They eat pancakes fried in lard, and drink hot tea with sugar. There's no shortage of water. Sloughs are everywhere, filled from the melted snow of winter.

After their lunch, Dido and Tato chop more trees for the building. Mama and Marusia dig around the stumps, preparing the soil for a garden. Andrei continues with the floor excavation. The shovelling was easy at first, the soil soft and leafy, but soon the spade hits roots that must be chopped and pulled out, and all the black soil must be cleared from the pit. Andrei's shirt is damp with sweat.

By early evening, the sun shines low in a cloudless sky and the *buda's* enclosed with poles leaning on each side, supported by the roof beam. Supper is a stew of dumplings and mushrooms. Maybe tomorrow Andrei can snare another bird. They sit around the fire, their clothes finally dry. The sun has dried last year's old grass, and tonight the family will have soft and dry beds under the spruce.

On the second day, they cut sod from a hillside. Dido and Tato slice through the sod. They peel it from the soil. The sods are three inches thick, four inches wide, and a foot long.

Dido says the roots hold together as well as any sod he's ever worked with.

Mama and Marusia lay willows horizontally across the *buda's* leaning roof, knotting them securely with thin lengths of green hazelnut branches. Andrei carries sods and he helps lay them on the roof, the first layer grass-side down, the willow keeping the sods from sliding off the roof, the second layer grass-side up. By this time, Tato and Dido are fastening the vertical poles forming each end wall. Tomorrow they will plaster the inside. Tato says they'll build an oven later. For now it's good enough to cook outside on the iron ring. In summer it's better anyway to cook outside.

The third morning, Andrei and Marusia tramp with bare feet in the pit filled with clay, chopped-up grass, and water. Mama and Tato stand themselves ankle-deep in the mixture, and they plaster the interior roof and end walls of the *buda.* Dido has started to dig a well beside the slough. By summer they will need a well. The water in the slough's fresh and clean right now, but by summer it will be stale, or the slough might even be dry by then.

By mid-afternoon the plastering's done. A woven blanket serves as a door. Andrei's dug two steps down from the entry to the floor of the *buda.* One more night they will sleep under the spruce. By tomorrow evening the clay will be dry enough for the family to sleep on the ledge inside the *buda.*

Andrei sets his shovel down and watches Dido struggling to climb out of the well he's been digging beside the slough. Bending forward, he rolls himself out, his arms extended flat out on the ground, his legs emerging after him, one at a time.

He crawls, then rises to his feet, both hands rubbing the small of his back.

"Water is seeping in already," he says as he approaches the *buda*. "I'm down four feet." He continues to the spruce tree, and crawls under the boughs. Andrei follows, to see him sorting through the belongings in his crate.

"Hey, *Pahn* Skomar!" Tato yells from the *buda*. "Isn't it about time you showed us what you're hiding in that bag?" He says this as Dido emerges from under the tree, the bag in his hand.

The family crowds around him. Andrei stands back at a distance, shading his eyes with his fingers, then rubbing his temple as if anticipating the onslaught of a spell. Mama makes the sign of the cross three times across her breast, then again three times at the goatskin bag. She must think that if it contains the Devil, the power of God will overcome.

Dido pulls out a box of polished wood, its lid carved with stars and crescent moons, clamped shut with a brass clasp. He lifts the lid and takes out an ornamented object wrapped in a black cloth. It's a cup. But not an ordinary cup. It's an ornate work of art, a treasure piece of crafted gold. The body of the cup is a circle of six horses, their heads reined in to the centre, the animals appearing to be running anti-clockwise as if in the frenzy of a whirlwind. A ruby the size of a walnut is set at the bottom of the cup, holding the reins. Andrei's mother repeats the sign of the cross.

The spell comes upon Andrei, and in his vision he's back at home in Ukraine. Forest has changed to meadow. Rainbow clouds lift. His family has vanished, and only the cup

remains, the golden halo, and the red sparkle, casting light in all directions.

The country's open to the sky. On the lush green meadow, the five Holochuk girls spring up like crocuses from the soil. They join hands and dance in a circle. On the bank of the stream, the homely Martha Shumka washes clothes. She dips an embroidered linen cloth into the water, rinsing then wringing it out. Andrei's dog Brovko runs back and forth from Martha to the girls, barking in a frenzy.

Natasha Holochuk steps out from the ring. She lays her embroidered linen cloth on an open patch of grass. At the edge of the field by the burial mounds, Cossacks on horseback form a single line. One rider breaks out from the formation.

Andrei sees himself tugging at the reins. All at once he kicks his heels and the horse gallops across the field. Andrei leans down the horse's side, his head mere inches from the ground. With his teeth he captures the linen and swings his body back upright on his mount.

As if a hand blots out the sun, the meadow clouds, air heavy with incense and striped the shaded colours of the rainbow, soon fade to a golden shimmer. Andrei hears a distant voice.

"A legacy of the Skomars?" his father asks.

The meadow's disappeared, the golden brilliance snuffed out to a red trickle of light inside the cup, a reflection of sunlight on the ruby.

Mama draws closer and picks it up, rubbing her fingers over the gold, turning the treasure round and round.

"Oi," she says, handing it back to Dido. "Can you sell it to Zitchka? And just look at Andrei. His face is white." She spits on the ground, and casts a derisive shove of her hand at the cup.

"It must be worth a fortune," Dido says, "but it's not to be sold."

"Not something to keep, either," Mama says. "It's no business of ours to mess with the Devil's handiwork."

Andrei remains with Dido, still watching the glint of the ruby. Dido quickly wraps the cup in its black cloth and puts it back in the box and into the bag. He makes a half turn, glancing back out of the corner of his eye. Andrei notices the glazed-over look, and he wonders what images Dido might have seen, or is the power given to Andrei alone?

"Last night I saw rabbits in the bush," Dido says. "I'm going to set snares." He takes an axe and two of Zitchka's iron nails with him.

"I'm going to help Dido with the rabbits," Andrei calls to his parents, and he runs to follow Dido before they can reply.

DIDO DOESN'T STAY IN THE BUSH. He walks about a hundred yards, then veers toward the trail that leads back to the river. Andrei stays just far enough behind that Dido won't notice him. They walk about a mile from the river to where a coulee begins its steep drop. A third of the way down the coulee's broad hillside, a large boulder protrudes skyward from out of the earth, from deep in a hole, a flat outcrop twice as wide as it is high. Far below in the coulee, along the bottom, a continuous tangle of grey and leafless poplar mingles with red willow, reaching down and down to the river.

Safely hidden in a clump of bushes covered with clusters of tiny white flowers, Andrei watches as Dido descends the hillside toward the rock. Dido drops into a hollow, standing still a long moment facing the rock, then slowly paces to one end, then back to the other. He peers around in all directions, then falls to his knees and makes the sign of the cross, all in one motion. Once back on his feet he disappears.

The minutes pass, a quarter of an hour or more, and finally Dido reappears from behind the rock. He no longer has the goatskin bag. Andrei watches as his grandfather descends further down to the stand of tangled poplars. He chops down a tree, trims off the top, and hacks a four-foot length from the bottom. He notches this piece and the main pole, and nails them together forming a cross. He lifts his creation to his shoulder, dragging it, disappearing further into the bush. What has the cup shown Dido? He's dragged his poplar cross away as if he were the Holy man Skomar himself.

Andrei remains hidden in the thick copse of bushes in the upper draw of the coulee. The brightness of the mid-afternoon sun and the chirping of chickadees has changed to the shadowy quiet of dusk. A lone hawk bobs in the sky's currents as finally Andrei approaches the broad face of the rock. It seems sunk into the earth, along its front a depression, a path worn deep into the ground. Andrei steps down into the hollow, where he has to stand on tiptoe to reach the top of the rock, and it's wide, extending from side to side at least twelve feet. He doesn't know how far it sinks into the earth. Its rust-brown face is worn smooth to a height even with Andrei's shoulders. Above that it's more abrasive, grown over here and there with lichens. There are several layers of horizontal cracks.

It seems almost alive, or else a long time sleeping, or slowly waking. The rock slants slightly upward, rising to the west, its crevices at this westward edge seeming to form lips and nostrils, a butt of a chin, creases in a face. It resembles an animal with a thick neck, the rock bulged with massive shoulders. It's so alone out here, as if stranded like a whale on land. At its eastward edge, the rock is cracked and slumped, weighted, it seems, with age. The colour is not a solid brown, but patched brown on beige and grey. Andrei paces like his dido, running his hand along the wall all the way to where he imagines the mouth formed from the open crack.

A glint catches his eye. Something shoved into the mouth. It's a brass button the size of a twenty-five cent piece. He's never seen anything like it before. Andrei puts the button in his pocket. He steps around to the back of the rock where it's not nearly so high, no deep depression, instead a few small rocks and scanty shrubs. He notices that the turf here has been disturbed, that Dido must have been digging and must have buried the goatskin bag. He gets down on his knees and moves stones out of the way. It's then he hears from somewhere behind him the shrill yipping of coyotes, a sound that jabs into the skin at the back of his neck. He turns his head, and out of nowhere, in a sudden roaring gust of wind, a swirl of black wings slaps down at him and then away.

The wind stops just as suddenly, and all at once there is no sound whatsoever, not the rustle of aspen leaves, not the hum of insects. A red ant crawls up from the base of the rock and Andrei imagines hearing a clatter of its tiny feet. Andrei digs at the disturbed turf, seaching for the bag. Then he does hear a clatter, the shaking of a rattle to his right and then his left. He hears a huffing, snorting, and grunting. He looks up and stares into the eyes of a black bear, upright, the claws of its front feet scraping at the rock, his head tossing from side to side, tongue drooling, teeth flashing. Andrei takes off running all the way to the top of the hill, never once looking back. Only when he thinks he's far enough away does he dare look. Far below, a crow circles then descends to perch atop the rock. The bear has disappeared.

May

CHAPTER 4

TATO AND DIDO HAVE BEEN GONE FIVE DAYS. ANDREI wonders if they made the walk to Klassen's farm all in one day. They left early enough in the morning, but would Dido have been able to keep going without stopping to rest? Maybe they caught a ride on somebody's wagon at the Fish Creek Ferry.

Andrei likes to think that Tato has left him in charge. Mama didn't think so. She had at first complained that she was being left in a wilderness, that there might be wolves and bears. She wept that she'd be left all alone out here with the children, and not a neighbour in sight.

"Andrei and Marusia are not babies," Tato had said. He insisted that he and Dido had to go. There was nothing else they could do.

If the Baydas were going to have a cow, a team of oxen, and a plow, there was no other choice. And so they had set out to walk the twenty-five miles back to Rosthern. With Dido needing frequent rest, it might take them all day and part of the next.

"Look after things," Tato had said. "Stay here, Andrei. Help your mother and sister. They need a strong man like you to help clear land for the garden. And finish digging the well. Dido says there will be more than enough water six feet down."

But surely, Andrei thinks, they will have caught a ride at the ferry...

A fancy buggy approaches on the trail into the yard. They have a visitor. Is he bringing news from Tato? Andrei runs to meet the buggy. The bay horse is sleek and muscled, with its colt of the same colour running loose beside. A cow is tethered to the surrey.

"You are Baydas?" The man is the opposite of the delicate sleekness of the horse and carriage. He's about forty years old, maybe forty-five at the most, short of stature, with a big stomach and thick neck, almost no neck, as if his head is a stone poking up from a prairie hill. His greying moustache is stained brown.

"I come from Wakaw," he says, "from my farm. How news travels, you know. I heard that a family had arrived from County Horodenka. Stefan and Paraska Bayda. I came five years ago from the same area." He gazes over Andrei's head. Mama and Marusia approach from the garden, both of them with hand on forehead, shielding their eyes from the sun.

"I am Wasyl Kuzyk," he tells Andrei. "Many know of me in these parts, but of course not here. Nobody lives here but you. This land was passed over."

The women stop by the *buda* and await the surrey's approach. Andrei skips along beside it with the colt.

"Glory to Christ!" says Wasyl Kuzyk in the traditional greeting. He looks over the heads of the women to the garden plot, and then his head makes a complete turn back to his cow tied behind the buggy. He takes a sudden glance at Marusia, covers his mouth with his hand and coughs, then addresses Andrei's mother. "Glory to Christ," he says again. "You must be Mrs. Bayda."

"Glory forever," Mama says, returning the greeting. She leans her hoe against the front wall of the *buda*.

"This is Mr. Kuzyk," Andrei says. "Everybody knows him."

"And your sister? What is her name?" the man asks, hands patting his knees.

"That's Marusia," Andrei answers him, at the same time attempting to pat the colt, but it skitters away.

"Marusia! That's a pretty name. Do you know that here in Canada they would say *Mary?*" He spouts these words like a schoolteacher, as if to show how much he knows about this new country.

"You have a family?" Mama asks. "A wife and children?"

"Oh," Mr. Kuzyk says, ogling Marusia, "I am still a single man. No time yet for marriage. But one of these days, if the right girl comes along."

Days in the field have only begun to weather Marusia's fair skin. She blushes, eyes to the ground. Andrei notices her discomfort. The visitor stares at her. She unties the knot in her white head scarf only to tie it all the tighter. Andrei can bet that Marusia's not saving her embroidered wedding scarf for this man who must be more than twice her age.

"I was wondering," Mr. Kuzyk says, shifting on his perch to sit upright, hands on his knees, "people I know from Horodenka tell me that Danylo Skomar arrived with you. Is that not true, Mrs. Bayda?"

"He is my father, and he lives with us."

"Many from Horodenka knew Danylo Skomar. He still plays the willow flute? Still tells stories?"

"Is there time for such things in this country?" Mama asks. "The men are away working."

"I was wondering," Wasyl says again. "I notice you have no chickens."

"Where would I get money for chickens?"

"I have an extra setting hen. Hens setting all over the yard...in the barn loft, the bush. They have nests all over the place." He reaches back in the buggy and hands Andrei a straw-lined box filled with eggs, and then a burlap sack containing the hen. "I bring it to you, Mrs. Bayda, and next year when it has raised its brood, you can return a hen."

"A hen? *Oi, oi.*" Mama swipes dust from her apron. She bobs forward and back, as if in a swoon, as if she's about to bow her head to the ground at Mr. Kuzyk's feet. "We could use chickens, but you don't have to..."

"And a cow," Mr. Kuzyk says.

"And a cow!" Mother's hands go to her face. She crosses herself. "Glory to God!" she says.

"The wolves took her calf, so now there's too much milk for just me and my mother. We are milking three others. You might be able to use a cow?"

"I tell you, we have no money."

"Pay me later, when you can. Take it off my hands. It's all right. Go, boy. Take it. Untie it."

"Oi, oi," Mama says. "*Dyakuyu!* Thank you! Thank you! Come in to our *buda* for tea, Mr. Kuzyk." She points toward the shelter. "Marusia. Go. Cut some cornmeal cake."

"No, it's all right, Mrs. I have no time. No time. Thank you. Thank you, anyway. I have to be on my way. My mother is waiting with my dinner. I don't want to be late."

Wasyl Kuzyk turns the surrey around and then taps the reins on the horse's rump, all the while taking one last look at Andrei's sister. "Glory to Christ!" he says once again, and drives out of the clearing onto the trail through the bush.

Andrei whispers to Marusia. "Do you think he's nice looking?" He runs into the bush as she picks up a stick.

"Don't you be so stupid," Mama says. "What if he turns around and sees you? A cow," she says to herself. "As if from heaven, here we are all at once with a setting hen and a cow. What will Stefan say when he sees us with a cow?" She holds on to its rope, and stares off in the direction of Mr. Kuzyk's disappearing buggy.

CHAPTER 5

ANDREI HADN'T DARED TO GO BACK TO THE ROCK BY himself, and with Dido away there is no one to ask. He wouldn't ask him anyway. It will have to be on Dido's invitation that Andrei goes back. The rattles frightened him. He doesn't know if they were snakes or what. But mostly he was frightened by the bear. Could it have been something to do with the cup? Somebody will have to be with him if he ever goes back to find out.

All tasks in Canada are ten times larger, the land ten times bigger, and Andrei is depended on to do the work. Mama said they must hurry with a garden if they want to survive the winter. It seems like he spends weeks pulling roots and picking rocks from the garden plot. When he tires from garden work, he and Marusia chop trees for a barn. They will build it as big as, if not bigger than, the *buda,* only he won't have to excavate the floor. A cow would never step down into a pit. It's simple enough to tamp in the two end posts, simple for him and Marusia to lift the roof beam in place, simple to lean posts against the beam for the slanted roof. They don't worry about sods; instead they will thatch the roof with grass. With the warmer days, mosquitoes will come, Mr. Kuzyk says. He says that soon during the early evenings they will be unbearable. It will be good to have a shelter for the cow. It won't be mosquito-proof, but a hay-covered barn is better than nothing. Andrei can set a smudge close by, as long as he doesn't set the barn on fire.

When he's not barn building, he's helping with the finishing touches to the *buda*. Mama has made the *peech,* the clay oven, against the end wall. Andrei helped her weave its willow frame. Then she plastered it with the best of clay, inside and out, making its walls six inches thick, even thicker on its broad top where Andrei sleeps. The floor is glazed shiny black with a mix of fine clay, soot, and wet cow manure. Using the drawknife, Andrei has made a door from poles, and he's fitted the pane of glass they brought from Rosthern. A week before the Green Holidays, the *buda* is finished.

After all this work, Andrei has an urge to explore, to see if he can seek out Gabriel and Chi Pete at the river crossing, about four miles away. Andrei wishes to find things out about cowboys. When the family came on the wagon over a month ago, he had noticed the horses penned in a corral at the river crossing, the team that Chi Pete led to the ferry, one horse named Raven and the smaller one, Crow. Gabriel's hat had reminded Andrei of a poster on the wall in the Winnipeg immigration hall. It showed a cowboy on horseback, wearing a black hat just like Gabriel's. Dido Danylo had asked the interpreter what the writing on the poster said: *Cowboys Ride the Range in the Last Best West!*

"I'm going to check the rabbit snares," he tells his mother. Andrei sets out on the grassy trail winding through the bush. He's not all that sure how far it is to the river crossing. He's not even all that sure how far it is to the rock. Did he have his eyes shut tight the evening he ran home? And the day they arrived, the day the Baydas rode on the wagon to the homestead, there were so many new things to see that Andrei didn't pay attention to the distance. He wonders, if he walks all the way, and meets up with cowboys and horses, will it be dark before he gets there and back home?

Tato and Dido Danylo have been gone a long time. When they get back, they'll be surprised to see how big the garden is. And what about the cow? Won't they be surprised to see the cow, a barn built for it, all mudded and everything. Andrei's mother wonders if they should start cutting hay. Should Andrei leave word at the crossing that they have a cow? Who could he tell, who would understand the Ukrainian language, and how would the news get to Tato? He could tell Gabriel. Andrei can't walk all the way to Rosthern to tell the Jewish merchant. What if Tato buys a cow? He said he would, and then they'd have two. Will the barn be big enough for two cows and a team of oxen?

The fresh green grass has grown above his knees. Poplar saplings, bursting with green foliage, rise up here and there above the grass, the sign of Pentecost, the glory of the Green Holidays. Year after year leafy branches graced every doorway in their village. But it was a chore getting them. Here you can't walk ten feet anywhere without the brushing of green branches. It's already June in Canada, but you can't change the calendar for the Holy days of the church. "Let the English be two weeks ahead with their Roman Calendar," Mama said, "but Pentecost is on Pentecost. Nobody can change that."

On each side the forest looms skyward, Andrei's eyes penetrating through walls of trees into darkness, and he feels a mosquito sting his forehead. He swats, blood splatters on his fingers. A squirrel skirts up a tree trunk, chattering, while higher yet a raven lands, black feathers ruffling, the branch bobbing up and down, sunlight blinking. The bushes sing with the chirping of birds. In open spots, bees hum in the pink patches of prairie roses. It seems that the very air droops with the sweet scent of aspen and rose.

Strawberries grow along the edge of the trees. Andrei stops to pick a few. He wishes he had something to put them in. The berries are small, but there are many, all of them sweet and full of juice. He's on his knees in the middle of the patch of berries. Mosquitoes hum in a cloud above his head.

He senses that he's not alone. He gets to his feet and hurries further down the trail to the open stretch that looks down on the hillside and the big rock. Something moves far below in the willows. He wonders if it is a deer. But then he's reminded of the shadowy figure he saw above the burial mounds the morning he saw the light. The same ghost-like movement of a black shadow, more the outline of a human figure than that of a deer. A minute later something else moves fluttering out of the branches, a crow swooping off to the east. And then from the west, a horse and rider appear.

From the distance, Andrei can't be sure, but the rider's

dressed the same as the young man who brought them on the wagon to the homestead. As the horse climbs the hill, getting closer, Andrei can make out his features. It is Gabriel. Andrei waves, and the large black horse bobs its head up and down, as if it's doing the answering. Gabriel wears his cowboy hat. A red sash is tied around his waist, and he carries a rifle resting on the horn of his saddle.

"The Bayda boy," Gabriel says, when he reaches Andrei. "A long way from your homestead. Where are you headed?"

"Just out walking," Andrei says. "Are you hunting?"

"Jump up here on Raven."

Gabriel asks questions. He wants to know how Andrei's family is getting along. Have they built a house? Do they have a garden? He has talked to Andrei's father and grandfather when they crossed on the ferry on their way to work for Jake Klassen. He asks about Andrei's sister Marusia.

Andrei asks about Chi Pete. "He wants to pay you a visit," Gabriel says. "Would it be all right for him to come?"

"Can he? Of course! We could go hunting. Does he have a rifle?"

"We are all hunters," Gabriel says.

"Are you an Indian?"

"I am Métis," Gabriel says. "Both Indian and French."

"And you are a cowboy?"

"I suppose," Gabriel says.

"How come you speak Ukrainian so well?"

"Not well," Gabriel says.

"At least I understand you."

"I help Uncle Moise at the ferry. Ukrainians come through

nearly every day, and I try talking to them. Uncle Moise says he's too old to learn a new language."

"Does anyone live close by here?"

"Indians come and go," Gabriel says. "Nobody farming. Our cattle graze along the river."

"There's Indians?"

"Lots north of here at the Reserve. But in the summer they like to travel. They follow a trail along the river to Saskatoon and farther south. It used to be a lot farther when there were buffalo."

"Did you hunt buffalo?"

"Not me, but my father remembers."

"Where are the buffalo?"

"All of them shot," Gabriel says.

"Will they ever come back?"

"No," Gabriel says. "It would need a very strong medicine to bring them back."

Gabriel gives a short tug on the reins and the horse stops. Hidden part way into the willows, a red rag is tied to a branch. "He's been here," Gabriel says.

"Who?"

"Snow Walker."

"Just because of that piece of cloth, you think somebody has been here?"

"Snow Walker leaves signs."

"Why?" Andrei gazes around in every direction.

"One of his tricks," Gabriel says. "He's a spirit man who lives alone."

"Why is he called Snow Walker?"

"It is said that he predicts the coming of bad weather. Some even say that he can cause it to happen."

"Is he a Métis?"

"Cree of the One Arrow people. But he lives at the river by himself, as if watching out for the arrival of intruders."

"Will he do something to us?"

"We'll just move along. Go about our business. He'll appear to us if he wants to, but probably not."

"You've seen him?"

"A few times. I can recall once, many years ago. I was on a horse with my father, just like you are with me, but I was much younger, on this very trail. I remember them talking, and many times after my father would tell the story at gatherings. He'd talk about Snow Walker to scare us children, and the old people would laugh. They said he could turn himself into a bear. He is very wise."

"He doesn't really turn himself into a bear," Andrei says. "How could he do that?"

"Perhaps just stories to scare children," Gabriel says. "But Snow Walker is real, all the same. On this very trail he and Father talked about the English soldiers stealing the church bell from Batoche. My father thought this was an evil act. Snow Walker didn't think so. He said the bell was bad medicine of the black robes and it was just as well it was gone."

They ride through the woods in silence. When they come across an animal's bed, Gabriel dismounts. It's a mere impression in the leaves that Andrei would not have noticed by himself. Gabriel presses his palm to the bed.

"Fresh."

"Is it a deer?" Andrei asks.

"Too large. Moose, I think. See the gouges? The leaves disturbed? We scared him up."

They walk for two hours, Andrei leading the horse and Gabriel scouting the tracks, spotting a broken twig here, and there the spots of uprooted turf on the forest floor. Then Gabriel stands still, one hand upright signalling Andrei to stop, the other hand holding the rifle. All is silent, but then a muffled cough sounds from somewhere close. Andrei sees no further than ten or fifteen feet into the trees.

Another cough and Andrei senses the direction. Gabriel aims the rifle, the shape of moose antlers slowly forming out of a tangle of twigs and branches. The rifle fires. A thud, a grunt, and a crash of trees.

The moose kicks, legs a frenzy in its death throes.

Andrei can't believe this. In Ukraine such events were for the sport of the Polish landlords, not the people. Even the rich would never have hunted an animal this big. Gabriel stabs its throat and the blood pumps out in spurts. He cuts out the tongue, slices a tip off the end and tosses it into his mouth.

"Try some?" Andrei shakes his head. Gabriel laughs, hands the tongue to Andrei, then rolls the moose onto its back. He grabs the antlers and twists the head to the side, bracing it against the animal's shoulder. Andrei sets the tongue down on a patch of grass then holds on to a back leg.

Gabriel slices the hide from the animal's neck down to its pelvis. He skins with the tip of his knife, pulling the hide away from the flesh, carefully spreading it on the forest floor.

Soon the carcass lies bare on its own blanket. Now he cuts through the flesh, from top to bottom.

Gabriel hands Andrei a hatchet. "Cut branches," he says, "and lay them in piles. Many branches."

Hands red with blood, Gabriel draws out the entrails. He gives Andrei the heart, kidneys, and liver to lay on the branches, then hands him his fire-blackened tea can.

"Get water from the creek," he says.

"Where?"

"That way through the trees," he says, pointing ahead. "Not far, maybe thirty yards."

When Andrei returns, Gabriel is turning intestines inside-out, the dung pellets plopping to the ground like marbles. He scrapes the intestines with his knife, then swishes them in the can of water.

"They are good to eat roasted," he says.

The paunch is swelled up like a balloon. Gabriel punctures it and a puff of foul air escapes. He slices open one of the four stomachs.

"Take the bible to the creek," he tells Andrei. "Rinse it out. Everything."

"The bible?"

"That's what my mother calls it. Clean out everything, then rinse. Swish the bible back and forth in the water."

It's like a ball split open, filled with vegetation piled layer upon layer, like pages, the membranes less than half an inch apart, covered with countless tiny nodes. Andrei runs with it, gets to the creek, and submerges the stomach. He works the linings with his fingers, all the time sloshing the bible up and down, and around and around in the water. After half an hour of this, he takes it back to Gabriel.

"Good job, Andrei. It's no small task to clean up the bible. It's my mother's favourite part of the moose. She will say a prayer for you."

They stack meat in piles. Gabriel tells Andrei to lay out more branches. The meat is stacked in this way...a layer of branches then a layer of meat, a layer of branches...meat...

"We'll take it to your place," Gabriel says. "Your mama might like to have some."

He and Andrei pack the cooled meat on the hide blanket, enclosing it by tying up the hide, first the front legs, then the back. The horse then drags the moose meat like a sled through the bush to the trail, and another mile to the Bayda farm.

Andrei can't wait to hear what Mama will say. He sees her and Marusia standing behind the willow fence they are weaving to enclose the garden. Mama draws her hands up to her face, eyes fixed on the horse and the parcel dragging behind. Marusia glances this way and that, but each time returning to Gabriel. She brushes dust from her clothing, clutches her dress and apron, shaking them.

"My friend," Andrei says. "Remember, at the ferry? He brought us here on the wagon. Remember Gabriel? He wants to give us some meat."

"Too much," Mama says.

"Not all of it," Andrei says. "Just a little. Just what his horse can't pack home."

Gabriel gets Andrei started in building a smoking rack, cutting willows and tying them, forming frames on tripods.

He opens the hide and starts preparing the meat. Marusia and Mama watch carefully. He slices the meat in sheets, like red rags, cut with the grain and not against it, so thin you can almost see through it.

Marusia runs to the *buda* and returns with a sharp knife. She kneels on the ground beside Gabriel.

"Sure," he says, "you try it." He takes hold of her knife hand. She glances up to him a moment, half questioning about the task, and half absorbed in the deep brown sparkle of his eyes.

"Keep it thin and even," he says. With their left hands holding the meat, he grips her right hand with his and guides the knife slicing into the red flesh. Andrei stands behind them holding a length of willow.

"I think I know what to do," Marusia says. "I can show Mama."

"Yes, Mr. Jarlay," Mama says, watching from a distance. "You go help Andrei. I will help Marusia."

"Sure," Gabriel says, patting Marusia's hand. "Remember, keep it thin."

He helps Andrei finish the racks, then they gather punky wood and willow saplings for the smudge fire. Gabriel lays a thin red blanket of moose meat on one of the poles, each side hanging downward to the smoke. As Mama and Marusia hang meat on the racks, Andrei helps with what Gabriel's taking home. They pack meat and entrails in hide bundles, two together, hanging them over the horse's back.

"Before you go," Mama says, "You eat."

Andrei draws water from the well and the two hunters

wash the dried blood from their hands and arms. Marusia prepares the place for their dinner. She spreads a blanket close enough to the smudge to keep the mosquitoes away. While Andrei builds a cooking fire and Gabriel brushes his horse, Marusia and Mama prepare the food, some of it in the *buda,* and some of it taken from the coolness of the well. Cottage cheese, butter, sour milk, cream, fresh bread, a stew of wild mushrooms, strawberries, the tea kettle and pot, a bottle of clear spirits Mama has taken from the trunk, and a small glass.

"Come Mr. Jarlay," Mama says. "You try this." She pours the liquid into the glass. Gabriel swipes the dust from his trousers, and with a flair bends down on one knee.

"What is your saying?" Gabriel asks, lifting the glass, making it sparkle in the sun. "To God?"

"To God," Mama says. "Yes, to God."

Andrei watches Gabriel sip and blink his eyes. He sips a second time then downs the rest, handing the glass back to Mama.

"More?" she asks.

"No," Gabriel says. "No. No." Marusia offers the plate of bread and he takes a crust, biting into it. The water in the kettle boils and Mama pours it into the teapot, making room on the iron cooking ring for the mushroom stew.

Gabriel sits back and lights his pipe. "Not so long ago," he says, "our people hunted buffalo."

"And didn't the Indians?"Andrei asks.

"Yes, Indians. They hunted buffalo for centuries. The animal was their food, clothing and shelter."

"And didn't Indians live in tents made from buffalo skins?"

"Yes, Andrei. Tents made from the tanned hides. And Indians showed the Métis how to make pemmican. The Métis then made tons of it. Dried the meat like you see smoking now. Most times, when the weather was hot, they dried it in the sun." Gabriel puffs on his pipe. He takes it out of his mouth and rubs his fingers along the stem. He frowns, his brown eyes appearing deep in thought, squinting, his tongue wetting his lips. Then he puffs again, two, three times.

"They'd pound the meat to a powder. Mix it with berries and fat. They packed the pemmican in cases made from rawhide, three feet long, two feet wide. Sold it to the Hudson Bay fur traders and to the freighters carting trade goods from St. Paul to Edmonton. They sold the hides to factories at Pittsburgh in the United States. They made belts out of them to run the engines in the steel mills."

"You know a lot." Andrei gazes at Gabriel's black hat, its wide and flat brim spread like a disk beside the toe of his moccasin.

"My father told me. He said that our people were wealthy. And now, after the buffalo are all gone, we pick up the buffalo bones and cart them to the station in Saskatoon."

"What for?" Andrei asks.

"They are shipped to the States for fertilizer. Or they use them to make gunpowder. Now there's no bones left."

Andrei stares at Gabriel, watching the smoke curl up from his pipe.

"Here, let me show you something." Gabriel gets to his

feet and walks to a clump of willows, cutting four saplings. He takes moose meat from a pack on the horse and brings it to the cooking fire.

"When we hunt, we roast our suppers on a stick. "

"Why don't we?" Marusia says.

Gabriel hands out the saplings and cuts the meat into four chunks.

Soon the meat is sizzling on sticks.

"Keep it away from the flames, Andrei!" Gabriel suspends the meat inches above glowing embers. "Like this," he says. The rich aroma of roasting moose meat holds everyone's attention.

"Ooh," Marusia says as she tears a strip of the cooked meat from her chunk and tastes the morsel, "is it ever good." She hands Gabriel a slice of buttered bread. Their fingertips touch, and their eyes meet, only for a moment. Andrei thinks that Gabriel likes his sister.

June

CHAPTER 6

ANDREI WAKES TO THE CHIRPING OF BIRDS, AND THEN HE hears something else...the creak of buggy springs and a sound like a dog whimpering. He looks out the window. Mr. Kuzyk tethers his horse to a tree, the colt nuzzling to his mama's flank. He unties a squirming gunny sack and a black-and-white puppy emerges, tumbling to the ground. It runs about the yard barking at the garden fence.

"It's Mr. Kuzyk," Andrei says in a hushed voice and scrambles into his trousers. He pokes his head out the door. "Mama and Marusia will be out in just a minute," he says.

"Don't bother them. I was just wondering if you could use a dog," Mr. Kuzyk says. "I'm taking cream and eggs to Rosthern. I thought, why not drop one of the pups off at Baydas."

The animal's belly sprawls flat to the ground and its tail wags. Head turns, nose twitches, then off the puppy scampers to the meat racks. He jumps at the strips of dried meat and falls over backwards. He sniffs a solitary curl of smoke that rises lazily from the spent smudge, all at once yipping and backing away.

A dog, Andrei thinks, and all at once he remembers Brovko. He didn't think that he'd ever wish to own a different dog after having to leave Brovko behind. He had even considered a visit to the talisman cup. Maybe it would have the power to call Brovko to Canada. But this puppy could be his twin. He even has hair falling over his eyes.

Mr. Kuzyk examines the meat drying on the racks.

"Try some," Andrei says, "and feed a piece to the puppy."

Mr. Kuzyk tears a strip and shoves a piece of it into his mouth. He chews a long time, finally swallowing the meat.

"Not bad," he says. "A good way to preserve the meat."

"Moose," Andrei says. "It's not ready until you can crack it in pieces." This was what Gabriel had told Andrei. He stirs the piles of ashes, exposing embers, and then he adds fresh willow and punk to the smouldering heaps.

"You shot a moose?"

"An Indian did." It's not really a lie. Andrei's friend said that he was part Indian. He is a cowboy and an Indian all in one.

Two white headscarves poke out of the door.

"Glory to Christ!" Mr. Kuzyk says.

"Glory forever," Mama answers, stepping out of the *buda*. Marusia follows directly behind Mama, partially hidden from Mr. Kuzyk's view.

"What brings you here in the morning?" Mama asks. She

talks so pleasantly, smiling at Mr. Kuzyk, then at Marusia, and back again at Mr. Kuzyk. Andrei hasn't seen her smile like that since last Easter when the priest admired the eggs and decorated bread in the basket she took to be blessed at church.

"I have an extra dog. You might have a use for a dog when you live out here all by yourself."

"Can I keep him, Mama?" Andrei picks up the dog. He cradles the puppy in his arms and rubs his ears. He lifts the hair from over his eyes. "See, just like Brovko." The dog licks the back of his hand. It hadn't been easy for Andrei to leave his old dog behind with Petrus Shumka. Surely Mama knows that. Surely she will let him keep this one.

"I have no money," Mama says.

"You don't pay money for a dog," Mr. Kuzyk says. "What can I do with a brood of pups? I drown them in a barrel."

Mama looks at the racks of moose meat. Her eyes soften as she pats Andrei on the top of his head. He steps back, runs his fingers through his hair, and lifts the dog to his face, letting it lick his cheek.

"Put it down, Andrei. I suppose..." Mama says, "we have enough to feed it."

"I can keep it? Another Brovko?"

"Stefan would like us to have a dog...what did I tell you, Andrei? Put the dog down." She smiles. "Mr. Kuzyk, come in to the *buda.*"

They sit on blocks of wood at the table, their old country trunk, drinking tea and eating pieces of corn meal cake, a special treat made from corn flour Andrei's father bought in

Rosthern. The dog pants at Andrei's feet. He pats its head and feeds it cake.

Mr. Kuzyk brushes crumbs from his moustache. He leans forward, eyes squinting at Mama, his eyebrows twitching. Andrei pokes Marusia with his elbow. Mr. Kuzyk's eyes meet Marusia's then quickly dart to the floor. A deep red blush rises from the base of his neck to his ears and nose. Andrei sees this and it's all he can do to keep from laughing. He coughs into his hands. Marusia passes Andrei a towel. "Use this," she says, then fidgets with the gathered hem of her sleeve.

"There is something, Mrs., something I haven't told you."

"Oh?" Mama says.

Andrei imagines from the strained look on the man's face that he is about to reveal a guarded secret. Somebody is sick, or else he has another gift. Maybe he has a storehouse full of gold and it's too much trouble for him to guard it. Of course not. Anybody with any sense can see that Mr. Kuzyk wants a wife and Mama wants a rich son-in-law. Andrei elbows Marusia once more.

"I can use some extra help on my farm." He straightens up, pulls on the chain of his watch and reads the time. He must be a busy man.

"Help?" Mama says, then touches her lips with her fingertips.

"Yes, there is only me and my mother. I don't know what I'll do when harvest comes."

"Maybe some of us can help. When Stefan gets back from Rosthern..." Mama pours him more tea.

"Somebody right now. You know, a man should have a wife."

Andrei kicks Marusia's foot and she kicks back. He catches her eye. All at once Marusia must think it's funny. Her head starts to shake and she buries her face in her apron. Mr. Kuzyk sips his tea. He glances at Marusia and sets the cup down, breaking into a fit of coughs, his eyes pinched and face strained red, finally pounding himself on the chest.

"I'm all right," he says. "Just a little congestion." He pulls a red and white handkerchief from his vest pocket and wipes his lips. "So much work, you know. This spring I purchased another quarter of land. From the Canadian Pacific Railway."

Marusia picks up the milk pail and takes one step for the door.

"Ah," Mama says, "you see? There she goes doing chores." Marusia stops. "I don't even have to tell her. With my Marusia to do the work, what is left for me?" She takes another step. Mr. Kuzyk is talking about a job.

"Of course, what is there left for you to do? But you know, maybe something can be done. Maybe the Good Lord has brought us together. I want my house cleaned for the Green Holidays. Someone to help my old mama whitewash the walls. She sent me to find someone to work. Do you know of anybody? I would help her myself, but there is hay to cut. Besides, I am cantor in the church and have to prepare for Pentecost."

"A church? There is a church?"

"Of course! We built it last summer. I donated two acres of land. The church is across the road from my house. In July the priest came from Winnipeg to bless it on the feast day of St. Peter. Maybe he will come again this year. I hope so. I hate to see the church empty, especially on a Sunday. I can go in to pray, but we need a priest if we are to have Mass. But you know, I keep an eye on the building, and when we do have a visiting priest, I am cantor." He smiles at Marusia. "Your daughter? She might clean my house? Everyone in the district knows that I can pay. Maybe both come. Maybe your son and your daughter. What do you say, Andrei? I'll show you how to start training a colt."

The colt. Andrei had forgotten. He'd give anything to own the colt. He'd quit teasing Marusia. He'd coax her into liking Wasyl Kuzyk. Of course they can both work for him.

"Oh, can we, Mama?" Andrei stands up and goes to the door, peering out. "We'll come home every night. Five miles is not far to walk."

"Hmmn." Mama places her hand on her daughter's wrist. Marusia's fingers grip white to the handle of the pail. Andrei sees his sister's dark eyes shooting darts at the farmer's hands, like hams plopped on his knees. She glances from side to side, and then with lips pursed, she bangs the pail against the doorpost, then shrugs and steps out of the *buda.*

"Sure," Mr. Kuzyk says. "Come this week. Get everything ready for the Green Holidays. Then for Saturday and Sunday you come too. Visit my mama. Meet everybody in the district at the Pentecost celebration."

Andrei runs outside, and in a moment is back inside with the puppy in his arms. "Brovko the Second," he says.

"Shoo!" Mama says.

"Brovko," Andrei says. "Don't you think so, Mama? We'll call him Brovko."

CHAPTER 7

"HE'S OLD," MARUSIA SAYS, AS SHE AND ANDREI WALK the trail to Kuzyk's farm. It's five o'clock in the morning, the sun just up, the air fresh and clean with no mosquitoes.

"And rich," Andrei says.

"And fat!"

"And he owns ten horses."

"He can keep them."

"But I think Mama wants you to marry him."

"I know, and if he asks, she will insist. What can I do?"

"Oh, Marusia!"

"And I'm changing my name. From now on call me *Marie.* We live in Canada now. No more *Marusia.*"

"*Marie?* Isn't that French?"

"I don't care. From now on my name is *Marie.*"

"Mr. Kuzyk says that *Marusia* is *Mary* here in Canada."

"Would you shut up about Mr. Kuzyk?"

"But if you stop and think, he's got a big farm, Mary."

"Didn't you hear me? Not *Marusia,* and certainly not *Mary.* From now on, for the second time I'm telling you, my name is *Marie.*"

"Hey, it's Gabriel. Is that it? No more Ukrainian boys. Not even Petrus?"

"Who's thinking about boys? Just call me *Marie.*"

"Mr. Kuzyk's older than a boy."

"I told you to shut up about him."

Andrei quits teasing for now. It used to be simple when there was only Petrus Shumka. Andrei liked Petrus as if he were a brother, but now there is Gabriel and he is not even of Andrei's people.

They march along the path, hurrying to keep ahead of the waking mosquitoes. Both are silent until Marusia chants to the rhythm of their walk. "Kuzyk! Kuzyk! Kuzyk!" Both of them burst out laughing.

"Oh, Marusia," Andrei says.

"I mean it," Marusia says. "From now on it's *Marie.*"

They come upon the church. It's built in the shape of a stubby cross, of planed lumber, and not of mudded logs like all the district's dwellings. A porch is attached, and above it, two arched windows look into the choir loft. It's a small church, but above, at the centre of the cross, a broad hexagonal structure is built into the roof. Andrei can visualize that, from inside the building, the roof shows the dome of the heavens and the spread of angel wings.

Across the road, Kuzyk's yard has everything in place. The barnyard is surrounded with corrals and the entire yard fenced with rails. The garden is protected from chickens and geese with a tightly woven willow fence. A large clay bake oven sits behind the house beside the neatly stacked woodpile. Every log building plastered with clay shows not a crack or sign of crumbling anywhere. The thatched roofs are thick and trim on all the buildings. The clay on the house walls has a rich tinge of blue.

An old woman as wide as she is tall stands bent at the well. She pulls a rope attached to a pulley, draws a pail of water, then turns to face Andrei and Marie. Half a dozen white geese waddle about her. Their beaks gape open, tongues vibrating a chorus of hisses. A gander nips at Andrei's pantleg and he swats its long neck with his cap.

"You come with me to work," she says to Marie. "Carry the water to the house. And you, boy. Go to the shed." She points to a building with an open door where Wasyl Kuzyk is sharpening a scythe on a grinding wheel. "My son is waiting for you."

The geese hiss once more at Andrei, all in unison. He steps back and swipes at them again with his cap.

"You don't hurt them," the woman says, jabbing the air with her finger. She starts for the house, Marie beside her with the pail, and the six geese, heads held high, waddling behind.

"So you came to work," Wasyl Kuzyk says. He holds his thumb to the blade of the scythe, rubbing carefully. "You can do anything if you have the right tools," he tells Andrei. "I will be busy here awhile. I want to sharpen ploughshares. Then I might take some time at the house. Mama and your sister might need me for something." He hands Andrei an axe and gazes in the direction of the house at the same time. "Your sister likes my farm, don't you think?"

Andrei shrugs his shoulders. "Where do I go?" he asks.

"To the breaking. You'll be fine working by yourself. Behind the barn. Follow the path through the bush. Half a mile, you come to a clearing. Pull roots and stack them in piles. What you can't pull, chop out with the axe. Oh, and here is something for mosquitoes." Mr. Kuzyk takes a medicine jar from his workbench shelf, and hands it to Andrei. "Put some on your face when you're out there. Work until you can't find your shadow, then come for lunch."

Poplar forest surrounds the breaking, and any breeze there might be is caught in the gentle ripple of leaves shimmering at the tops of the trees. As Andrei pulls at a root, mosquitoes swarm around his head. He ties a scarf over his ears, and tries to ignore them. He thinks about Snow Walker, and what would happen if all of a sudden he appeared out of the trees. Would Andrei know who it was, or might he think it was merely an ordinary Indian? He wipes sweat from his forehead and retreats to the edge of the breaking. He drinks from his jar of water, and rubs his face with the ointment. Dragonflies dart, then stop and dart again, their wings buzzing in the summer heat. A dozen red-winged blackbirds flit about the reeds at the edge of a slough. Ducks quack hidden in bulrushes, and crows rasp their unknown displeasure somewhere in the trees.

At noon Andrei trudges along the path through the trees

to the Kuzyk yard. He notices Marie at the well, bent over the water trough. Her linen smock and her headscarf are covered with blue splatters. She pumps water into the trough, then scrubs the bristles of a push broom. An unwashed hand brush sits on the well cover. A daub of the blue quicklime solution decorates the tip of her nose.

"Whitewash?" Andrei asks.

"The old woman added a full bottle of washing blue she bought from the Rosthern store."

"Rich like a *pahn*," Andrei says. The Kuzyks buy sacks of quicklime and bottles of washing blue, while if the Baydas want a finishing coat on a wall, they have to use the ash-grey clay Andrei digs from the swamp. But then it would be foolish to spend money on a *buda.* Maybe when they build a real house, Tato will buy quicklime.

"Kuzyk must have a lot of money." Andrei picks at a callous on the palm of his hand. "Wouldn't it be nice to farm if you had money?"

"Money isn't everything." She scrubs extra hard and glares at Andrei.

"He's a generous man," Andrei says, turning his gaze to survey the yard, the buildings, and the horses in the barn corral. Marie lifts the broom out of the trough and shakes it, showering Andrei's trousers with water. Just as she does this, the battalion of geese struts toward them, heads forward and extended on bent necks, tongues darting as if from the sneering mouths of snakes. Andrei dips a bucket of water from the trough and splashes the whole lot of them. They hiss once more then march away, just as if they've been horribly affronted, and they won't give as much as the time of day to these two offending intruders.

"He's an old man," Marie says.

"Forty. You should at least think about it." He points to all the buildings and the horses. "Look at this farm," he says, and then winks at her.

"Oh, for God's sake," Marie says, and she grabs the unwashed brush and throws it in Andrei's face.

"I give up," he says, laughing, and then he pulls out a handful of long green grass growing beside the well. The colt is standing with his head hung over the top rail. Andrei runs to it. He feeds it the grass and he rubs his hand down the colt's long nose.

LATER IN THE HOUSE, Mrs. Kuzyk gives orders. "We shouldn't waste time. After you eat, I want Andrei to cut poplar branches. Ones with lots of leaves. Wasyl will show you."

Andrei spoons sour cream into his beet *borshch*, smears butter on a thick slice of bread, and then eats non-stop. In ten minutes he's done eating and gone from the house, and soon runs back with an armful of branches higher than his head.

Marie places the greenery over the doorway, Mrs. Kuzyk pointing all the while. "And here, Marusia," she says. "The whitewash is dry enough." She points to the walls in the east room. "String them along the ceiling. And here, I'll show you." With more green branches Mrs. Kuzyk frames one of the icons on the wall. "All of the pictures."

"I know," Marie says. "We did the same with our house in our village."

"Don't forget," Mrs. Kuzyk says, "Bring your mother on Saturday."

"I know," Marie says.

Mrs. Kuzyk watches the way Marie arranges the branches, how she forms an arbour over the doorway. Marie doesn't notice this, but the old lady has been observing all day, and when she examines the arbour, she nods her head and smiles.

Mrs. Kuzyk has already planted kernels of wheat, barley, and oats in small pots, setting them on the sill of the window in each of the two rooms, and on the bench outside on the south wall of the house. These sprouts are for ornament and promise. Outside the wheat fields flourish in a sea of green. She stands in the centre of the east room, her plump arms folded across her chest. She surveys her finery, and Andrei senses what she's thinking. If her seeds grow in pots planted in the week of Pentecost, then surely the Kuzyk fields will be blessed, and maybe son Wasyl will be blessed as well.

SATURDAY THERE IS NO WORK because it is a church holiday. Saturday is the first day of the Green Holidays. Mama and Marie sit in places of honour at Mrs. Kuzyk's table amid the greenery in the east room. Andrei and Mr. Kuzyk sit within sight and hearing distance, playing cards at a small table by the door.

Mama presses her hand down her apron, smoothing out

wrinkles real or imagined, eyes Marie up and down to confirm that she too is presentable. "You have bluing in the plaster, Mrs. Kuzyk."

"I think it holds up better in the rain," Mrs. Kuzyk says. "It won't wash away as easily."

"How is your son's breathing?" Mama asks.

"It's the time of the year. The grass pollen is hard on Wasyl's congestion. But only this time of year. Everything's growing. Poor Wasyl's all plugged up. But he's strong otherwise. Like a twenty-year-old."

Mr. Kuzyk slams down a card. "Beat that!" he says to Andrei.

Mrs. Kuzyk gets up off her bench and Mama attempts to do the same. Marie watches.

"Sit, sit," Mrs. Kuzyk says. "The kettle will be boiling. I'll get it from the summer kitchen."

Mama gazes at the icons on the wall. She lifts a corner of the embroidered linen table cover. The chest is not built quite the same as the Baydas'. A metal hinge runs along the centre. There are two compartments. Mama lifts the lid closest to her and Marie swipes her hand across the table, pressing down on the linen and on her mother's hand.

Mrs. Kuzyk comes back into the room carrying a tray with a teapot and china cups, fresh cream and strawberries, thick slices of crusty bread and butter. She pours tea.

"Take some strawberries in your bowl," she says. "I picked them this morning. They are so sweet you hardly need sugar. You men have some too. Come and get it."

"After this hand," Mr. Kuzyk says. "I'm giving the boy a

good trimming. What do you say, Andrei?"

"I'm going to try and put a halter on the colt before I go back to the field."

"You'll need a halter first. There's one hanging in the barn. It might be a little big, but you can cut another hole in the buckle strap."

Mama fills her bowl and Marie's, adds a spoonful of sugar, and pours on thick cream. They both eat. Mrs. Kuzyk watches them.

"What about yourself?" Mama asks as she spreads butter on bread, for herself and for Marie.

"I had a big breakfast with Wasyl before you came." Mama smiles and Mrs. Kuzyk smiles back. "Maybe just a little," she says, and she fixes a bowl for herself, then dips bread into the mixture and eats. Not a word more is said until the bowls are empty, and then Mama says, "Good berries," then more silence. Both mothers look at Marie, who stares at her fingers, fiddling with her apron.

"Your daughter isn't getting any younger," Mrs. Kuzyk says.

"No," Mama says. "It's getting the time when a young woman starts looking for a husband."

"Someone to look after her."

Mama smiles, nodding at Marie as if the prayers for a daughter's future are about to be answered.

"I want the best for my Marusia."

"Oh, by all means," Mrs. Kuzyk says. "You know..." She pauses to fill their cups with tea, "I was wondering. It is about time for my son Wasyl to start thinking about a wife. Would you be so kind to have Marusia consider him?"

Mr. Kuzyk breaks into a fit of coughing, covering his mouth with his red and white handkerchief.

"Oh dear," Mama says. "Do you hear that, Marusia?"

"Of course I hear." She wipes her eyes with her apron, and under her breath she whispers, "And I want to be called 'Marie.'" Then she says, "Mama, you know what I think. You know Petrus..."

"Petrus? What good is Petrus across the ocean?"

"He said that someday he might come..."

"And if he should ever come to Canada, what will he have for you? The shirt on his back?"

"I want to talk to Tato first...and to Dido Danylo. I don't want to get married. Andrei?" Marie stands up and takes one step toward him.

She's asking him. What does Andrei know about marriage, about what's good or what's bad for his sister? One thing he does know is that Mr. Kuzyk knows his horses. Andrei glances at Marie just for a moment, their eyes meeting. He hunches his shoulders and diverts his gaze back to the table. He takes a card from the top of the deck. It's a deuce. Marie takes one more step forward, but Mr. Kuzyk starts rising from his chair. She steps sideways, then rushes past him out of the room and out of the house.

CHAPTER 8

THE HALTER DOESN'T WORK. THE COLT WANTS NO PART of it, and Andrei leaves from his week of work at Kuzyk's in a downcast frame of mind. It takes a visit from Chi Pete to cheer him up. Chi Pete shows up the day after Pentecost and stays for two days. His mastery of Ukrainian is remarkable. Throughout these months of May and June, Gabriel has been drilling him to the point where he's now able to converse with Andrei. The first afternoon of the visit, the two boys decide to roam the bush, hunting for signs of moose. Andrei isn't sure what they'll do if they see one; Chi Pete has come without a rifle.

"Gabriel thought I better not take it," Chi Pete says.

They approach an open area in the forest, a large meadow with expanses of head-high willow saplings covering half of it, trails running through. A regular moose pasture.

"Let's separate here," Chi Pete says. "Along each side, and we'll meet at the other end. If we're together, a moose might just stay ahead of us and we'll never see him. This way I might scare him to you, or the other way around."

Brovko scurries between them, sniffing, back and forth on the trails. Andrei's halfway around the meadow when the dog runs to him, then shoots off into the bush. In a few moments, Andrei hears a frenzy of barking. About fifty yards into the bush, the dog has stopped at the foot of a tree, where he stands on his hind legs yipping and yowling as if he has treed a cat.

A bear cub nestles on a branch twelve feet off the ground, tiny eyes peering down at the barking dog. Andrei thinks to knock it down from the tree. He grabs a length of deadwood from the ground and pokes at the cub. It turns its head and bites at the stick. Claws scrape against bark, paws curling to hang on.

"Chi Pete! Chi Pete!" Andrei yells. "Come quick! Over here in the bush!" Andrei thinks that he can capture the cub and take it home for a pet. He doesn't realize the cub might have a mama close by. Just as Andrei begins to shinny up the tree, he hears the growl, and the further-away voice of Chi Pete.

"Get down," Chi Pete says, "and walk away slowly. Back up, and keep your eyes on the bear's eyes." Andrei turns around to face the mama bear, twenty feet away. The dog runs to it, barking, face to face, as if protecting Andrei. The bear's paw swipes, rolling the dog in a tumble, hide torn open, whimpering. Chi Pete picks him up.

"Slowly," he says. They back out of the bush, step by step toward the meadow, the mama bear never taking her eyes from them, standing at the tree, under the cub. They make it to the meadow, and without words go on to the homestead where Mama can tend to the injured dog.

The next morning the boys work up enough nerve to head back into the bush, without the dog, who is at home nursing his wounds. They hunt for grouse. All morning they walk, finding nothing. By noon they arrive at the big rock. Andrei reaches into his pocket. "I found this button the last time I was here," Andrei says, "in one of these cracks."

"Let me see it." Chi Pete rubs the brass with his fingers. "It's from an army coat. Uncle Moise told me about shooting the redcoats at Fish Creek. Just down river from the ferry. Someone has left it here as an offering."

"You think so?" Andrei asks. He tells Chi Pete about the ghost he thought he saw earlier in the summer, moving in the willows at the bottom of the hill. It was a black shadow similar to the form he saw take the golden halo from around the cross on the burial mound at Zabokruky. He tells Chi Pete about the cup in the goatskin. "My dido has buried a talisman here. Should we dig it out?"

"What's that?"

"A gold cup," Andrei says. "Inside a bag. A Holy man sent it with us. It has a special power."

"We should leave it," Chi Pete says. "Your grandfather made an offering to the spirits. And maybe you should put the button back."

"No," Andrei says. "It's mine."

Chi Pete shakes his head. For a while he doesn't talk, and then he says that if it were up to him, he'd put the button back.

"Finders keepers," Andrei says.

They walk downhill toward the river, a quarter of a mile down the winding coulee. They step across a beaver dam. Saskatoon berries hang from branches.

"You know Snow Walker?" Andrei asks.

Chi Pete shrugs. "I think I know where he lives. Gabriel says he darts back and forth from the hills, haunting up and down the river."

The river bottom stretches wide. The channel snakes around broad stretches of sand, forming shallow pools. The boys swim, then lie drying on the hot sand.

"Snow Walker could be anywhere up from this shoreline," Chi Pete says. "In any of these coulees."

The boys enter one of the narrow breaks that's cut to the river. They follow a dry stream bed, the path of deer, coyotes, bears, and whatever other animals go down to the river to drink. Branches encroach from each side, here and there forming a canopy blotting out the sun. Willows grow, then farther up, chokecherry bushes, hawthorn, saskatoon, buffalo berry, and once in a while the gnarled figure of a red ash tree.

To Andrei's right, just off the trail, a fragment of red polka dot cloth dangles on a cluster of green chokecherries. All at once Andrei feels that he and Chi Pete don't have this trail all to themselves. Further ahead, a strip of dried meat hangs from a branch.

It's at this spot that they hear the rattle, first Chi Pete, then Andrei.

"Up there," Chi Pete says. They gaze squinting through leaves and branches up the side of the coulee, directly at the sun. Part way up, in the arms of a tree different from the others, its trunk and branches gnarled and twisted, the sound of a rattle comes from right in the middle of the glint of sunlight. The rattle sounds again. Then everything's silent. A chickadee lands on a leafy branch. It chirps then flits to another.

They walk ahead another twenty feet. Half a dozen crows squawk and fly in circles above the massive jumble of a stick nest. Andrei turns to look at the ground behind him.

"Chi Pete! Chi Pete!"

Feet in rubber boots straddle the path. Canvas trousers are belted at the waist with a frayed rope. A fire-scorched tea can hangs from the belt. A checked shirt is tucked in. Arms spread open a dark suit jacket. A cap of white weasel skin clings to black hair. A weasel head drapes on each side of the man's brow along the front of his ears. In his left hand, a rattle shakes. Attached with strips of rawhide to a red willow stick are four dewclaws from the front feet of a white-tailed deer.

He talks in Cree to Chi Pete. Then he whistles through his teeth and shakes his rattle at Andrei.

"Snow Walker wants to know about your grandpa, the old man with the rope of hair. He says to ask the Rope Head if he left the bag as a gift, or as a curse on the spirits? Has he given it to work for or against the spirit rock?"

Andrei stares, not knowing what to say. He notices that Snow Walker turns away, avoiding eye contact. He steps around to the other side of Chi Pete and whispers in his ear. He shakes his rattle again, walking in a circle around Andrei.

"Snow Walker wants you to tell the Rope Head not to

pray from his knees, casting spells at the rock. Not to make the crosses of the French Black Robes. If he does, Snow Walker will turn the mischief back on the both of you. He wants to know if the power inside the bag is meant to work with, or against the power of Snow Walker and the rock."

The next moment he's gone. Gabriel has told Andrei that Snow Walker was said to have the power to make himself invisible. But those were only stories the old people told during the dark winter to scare the children. Andrei's not sure what to make of it. In this summer forest, a deer can vanish just as quickly.

July

CHAPTER 9

On a muggy July day, late in the afternoon, Tato and Dido come home with a wagon and team. The air hums with mosquitoes. The oxen swish their tails. They turn their heads around, their tongues swiping with sudden jerks at their backs. A smudge pot hangs from the wagon pole, a tin lard pail filled with smouldering green grass and wood chips. Dido walks beside the oxen, going from one side to the other wielding a switch of leafy poplar, swatting mosquitoes off them and the animal trailing behind, a sway-backed horse with white hair down its brow and over its eyes. The wagon stops in front of the primitive grass-roofed barn.

"You've built a barn!" Tato says. "And what have we here?" Inside the open doorway, Marie is milking the cow.

"From Mr. Kuzyk," Andrei says. "She gives so much, we milk twice a day. I do it in the morning."

"Kuzyk? Who is Kuzyk?" From his perch on the wagon,

Tato leans downward and to the side, directing a question to his wife. "Where would you find money to buy a cow?"

"Do you mean Wasyl Kuzyk?" Dido asks. "We had a Wasyl Kuzyk in district Horodenka. One day five years ago at the market he was selling two horses. You remember Stefan? Could it be the same Wasyl Kuzyk?"

"Yes," Mama says. "He knows both of you. And we paid him nothing."

"How, *nothing*?" Tato asks.

"I told him we had no money. He said not to worry. He said to pay when we can. If it takes one year, two years. Maybe the cow will have a heifer calf. He could take the calf, he said."

Once inside the *buda,* Mama asks questions. "How much money did you bring? You didn't buy a plough? What good is an ox without a plough?"

"We spent it all. Don't you remember Sam Zitchka? I still owe him. He sold us the team and wagon. And two more bags of flour. This took all our money. Is there anything to eat?"

Andrei, Tato, and Dido sit around the big chest that serves as their table.

"Off with your elbows," Mama says, and she lifts the lid, reaching inside for a loaf of bread. "Cream, Marusia. Go to the well. And cottage cheese..."

"I might get a horse," Andrei says. "Wasyl Kuzyk's favourite mare has a colt. You should see it, Dido."

"Oh?" A mosquito buzzes in circles over Dido's forearm. He waits until it lands, watches for a moment, then swats it.

"A magnificent horse? Fit for a Cossack prince?"

"A colt?" Tato asks. "And how will you pay for it? We don't need a fancy horse. Now, a draft horse would be something else."

"I worked for Mr. Kuzyk," Andrei says. "Marie and I can go back later at harvest time to stook."

"Marie?" Tato asks.

"She changed her name. She doesn't want to be called *Marusia.* She wants to be more Canadian."

"Oh? And you say Wasyl Kuzyk wants the both of you at harvest time? Who will help Mama?"

"What's to harvest?" Andrei says. "Vegetables. The only grain is one small plot of wheat and barley, to save the seed for next year."

"Mr. Kuzyk comes here often," Mama says. "He is rich like a *pahn* landlord."

"Dido and I will be going back to Klassen's for harvest. Maybe then I can buy the plough. Maybe pay the rest of our debt to Sam Zitchka. Wasyl Kuzyk's cow might have to wait."

"Mr. Kuzyk's in no hurry for money," Mama says. "And look what your daughter is serving you."

Marie sets down a bowl of moose jerky stewed with mushrooms, cream, and green onion tops. She serves cottage cheese, bread and butter, and a pitcher of thick sour milk. Andrei watches as Tato takes mouthful after mouthful of stew. He observes the slight trace of a smile on Tato's lips.

"Give Dido a piece of the dry meat," Andrei says. "Remember Gabriel the wagon driver? He came hunting here. We shot a moose. We cut it up. We made a smudge fire here in the yard to smoke the meat and dry it."

Dido chews and chews. He doesn't have many teeth, making his lips, chin, cheeks, and moustache roll around in circles. Finally he swallows.

Andrei wants to know about Dido's horse. It's not much of a horse...more like a plug when compared to Kuzyk's colt.

"Where did you get that horse?"

Dido dips a piece of bread into his plate of mushrooms, mopping the food to his mouth.

"I got it from the Mennonite. I put new shoes on four of his draft horses and he gave me Frank."

"Frank?" Andrei asks. "That's a horse's name?"

"Frank. That's it," Dido says.

"How old is he?"

"Old enough. Just like your Dido." And he sops up more of his mushrooms.

"How long are you home for?" Mama asks. "Will the house get built before winter, or will we have to live in this cave?"

"We have until stooking time," Tato says. "Three weeks. We can start squaring logs. When we leave, you and the children can square some more. Can't you, *Marie?*" Andrei's sister can't help but grin at the sound of her new name coming from Tato.

"Marusia has something to ask you," Mama says.

"No, I don't."

"Marie? Marusia?" Tato turns his head toward his daughter, who is standing in the dark corner by the clay stove, as far away as possible.

"She has the opportunity to be a *pahnia.*" Mama wipes

crumbs from the table, under their very noses.

"Kuzyk?" Tato says. "He gave us a cow."

"You have to pay for it," Marie says.

"That's true. If not now, some time in the future."

"Some time in the future he could even be dead. He's always coughing. By his looks, he must be older than you are, Tato."

"But a cow...?"

"And the colt," Andrei says. "He's more than four months old. Mr. Kuzyk says that whenever I have time I can be training it. He says by Christmas time I might teach it to pull a sled. By next spring I can take a thirty-foot rope and run the horse in a circle. He might even grow big enough by then for me to get on his back."

Tato wipes his moustache and laughs out loud, all at the same time. "That would be some trade. A young bride for Kuzyk in return for a horse. Who knows what this Kuzyk might do? If we hold out, he might toss in a breaking plough."

In her dark corner, Marie curls down to the floor. She buries her face in the folds of her apron and sobs.

"Don't cry," Tato says. He reaches out to her, but she shrinks from his touch. "Oh, Marie. You never know. Maybe Petrus Shumka will sail to Canada. Maybe he will buy a horse and ride into our yard like a Cossack prince. He will sweep you into his arms and race away."

"A Cossack," Dido says. He takes up his flute. Stroking it once, he puts it to his mouth and plays. He sounds the notes to an old song, making the music light and happy. Then he sets the instrument down and sings these words to the tune of the Hetman Bayda:

Petrus I love, love him so well
But I'm afraid, afraid to tell!
Oh, the trouble he gives with eyes so bright,
Black moustache and skin so white!

Marie wipes tears, glancing up at her grandfather.

"Don't be so silly, Dido." And then she pouts with her lips, sticks out her tongue, and finally smiles. Even Mama smiles, and out in the yard, Brovko barks and yips.

"Someone's here," Andrei says, and he rushes to see who it is. Standing out by the shallow well is the black horse Raven. He neighs, tossing his head up and down. Gabriel Desjarlais pats him on the neck and dismounts.

CHAPTER 10

"It's Gabriel." Andrei holds the door open. "Dido! Tato! Gabriel is here. He hunts moose, and he showed me how."

"How many times have you told us already?" Tato says. He sits at the table with Mama standing at his shoulder. Marie backs off to a dark corner where Dido sits on a stump, carving something from birchwood.

"Come in, come in," Tato says. "Close the door, Andrei. Before the mosquitoes eat us."

"Humid," Gabriel says. "You could cut the air with a knife. Nothing better, for mosquitoes." He holds his wide-brimmed hat in his hand.

"Sit. Sit down here," Tato says. "Hey, Marie. Bring a dish of mushrooms for Gabriel. You'd like a small drink, maybe?"

"I could rub it on my face to keep the mosquitoes away."

"Or make them drunk. Come on," Tato says, "a drink to your health."

"A little one," Gabriel says.

Mama takes the sealer of whiskey down from the shelf and sets it on the table. Tato pours a small glass.

"To God," Gabriel says. He drinks then coughs into his hand.

"To God," Tato answers, as he pours half a glass for himself. "How is the ferry business? I didn't see you this morning."

"We're selling our place at Fish Creek."

"Selling it? Why would you sell?"

"My father is selling it. He wants to be closer to our people. Even Uncle Moise has moved north. He's running the ferry now at Batoche. I shouldn't say this, but he thinks there are too many of your people coming to Fish Creek. He wants to be closer to the French at Bellevue."

Marie's hand shakes as she pours tea into tin cups. Mama slices more bread. "Go ahead," she tells Gabriel, pushing the pitcher of sour milk toward his plate. "Eat! Eat! And some of your moose meat."

"So what brings you here to our mosquitoes?" Tato asks.

"The day we were hunting," Gabriel says, smiling at Andrei, "I promised your son I'd take him to the fair, to the St. Joseph Celebrations at Batoche. Two weeks from last Sunday." Gabriel glances at Marie. "As a matter of fact, maybe your daughter might like to come along with us."

Mama swipes up crumbs. "St. Joseph's Day? Isn't that in the spring? At our village church, St. Joseph's Day was celebrated early in the spring."

"Louis Riel changed it," Gabriel says. "All the people are at the Batoche celebrations every year on the twenty-fourth of July. Mr. Letendre's birthday."

"Who is Mr. Letendre?" Tato asks.

"One of our leaders," Gabriel says. "His nickname, *Batoche.* And the settlement is also named *Batoche*. So the celebrations are held on his birthday. And then Louis Riel must have thought, why not celebrate St. Joseph's Day when all the people are already there? Louis Riel was a very religious man."

"And he could change the dates for the Holy Days of the Church. Just like the Roman calendar does with Pentecost," Mama says.

"Don't forget Easter," Tato says.

Mama frowns and directs Marie to clear the dishes from the table.

"There's even a midway," Gabriel says. "Prince Albert Fair was on Saturday. They had an outfit from the States and it's coming to Batoche. Monkeys and everything."

"Can I go? Can I go?" Andrei asks. "Dido, say it's okay."

"Why are you asking Dido?" Mama says. "It's not up to him."

"I can be here to get them," Gabriel says. "In twelve days. At dawn Sunday morning. We want to be on time for Mass and the procession of the banner of St. Joseph. The Adoration of the Holy Sacrament. In the afternoon there'll be horse races and foot races." He turns his full attention to Marie. "They have craft displays...crochet work, embroidery, hooked rugs, sashes..." Then he takes notice of Dido Danylo in the corner by the clay stove, still carving on his piece of birch. "They have tug-of-wars, firearm shooting, arm wrestling, music, and dancing." Gabriel stands and walks to the door. "I can't stay long. We're not finished putting up hay. So what do you think? In twelve days?"

Tato shrugs his shoulders and glances at Mama.

"We have no money to spend playing games," she says. "No money for monkeys."

"They don't need money," Gabriel says. "Who knows, Andrei might even win some at the foot races."

There is no stopping Andrei. He can't sit still. He will beg until his parents have to give in. He will run off without permission. He will go to work for Wasyl Kuzyk and nobody can tell him what he can or can't do.

"It would be an adventure," Dido Danylo says. "I might even jump on Frank and go see for myself."

"We are squaring logs," Mama says. "For the new house tomorrow, remember?"

"Marusia," Tato asks, looking at her, then over to his wife, "do you want to go?"

"It might be fun," she says. "I haven't been anywhere. I hilled the potatoes yesterday..."

"The cranberries have to be picked," Mama says.

"Mama," Marie says, "for goodness sake! Have the cranberries even finished blooming?"

"But two weeks from now?"

"Green," Tato says. "Highbush cranberries are better picked after a frost in the fall. You know that, Paraska." She has to nod her head, only slightly, but she has to nod all the same. Highbush cranberries are not something new to her. Not new to anyone who comes from Ukraine. She's even said in teasing that highbush cranberry trees and mushrooms are the only good reasons a person has to stay in this godforsaken land.

THE AWAITED SUNDAY MORNING ARRIVES. Now that they're finally on the trail, the scent of poplar both calms and excites Andrei. He rides in the back of the Desjarlais buggy, Raven harnessed to the traces. High up in the trees a slight breeze and fresh clean sunlight alter the leaves from green to silver.

"The Cree call these trees *noisy leaf,*" Gabriel says. He wears a buckskin jacket with fringes on the sleeves, and five brass buttons. Down the front on each side of the buttons runs a beadwork flower. The long stems are black, with green leaves sprouting the whole length, and coloured petals, some red, some a light blue. Another flower with the same colours is beaded on his breast pocket. Andrei's glad that his sister has dressed up.

She wears a red skirt embroidered white, green, yellow, and black in a broad strip along the bottom...squares and stars, flowers and wavy lines. Her black half-apron is tied at the waist with a knitted sash of white, black, and grey. Her full-sleeved white blouse gathers at her wrists and at the neck, and is embroidered just below each shoulder. Five strands of coral beads drape to her bustline. On her head is a black velvet tight-fitting cap embroidered all over with red flowers, and bordered all around with a silver-grey ribbon. Marie's complexion, tanned from working in the garden, has a golden-brown hue somewhat like Gabriel's. Her face is round and full, with red lips and straight white teeth, deep brown eyes the colour of her hair, and out on this adventure she wears a smile that makes her all the more beautiful.

But best of all her apparel are the moccasins, red-dyed soft leather, that ride halfway to her knees. Gabriel brought them this morning as a gift. His mother makes them. She boils the bark of red willow to give the leather its colour. She wins prizes for her work and she will have moccasins, beaded deerskin coats, and sashes on display at the fair.

When they reach Fish Creek, they follow the trail which runs north along the river. For most of the way, the deep green billows of shrubs and walls of poplar forest block Andrei's vision, but once in a while the foliage breaks away to open stretches of grass. Here he sees far down to the winding blue ribbon of water. Across the river, the lush green pillows of forest roll up the west bank. A grey haze shimmers through these green banks. In these moments of open prairie and far horizons, Andrei's spellbound. In his village he could look away to the foothills of the Carpathians, but here the landscape spreads forever. Even the mosquitoes are bearable, but Gabriel has a smudge pail ready just in case.

Closer to Batoche the open spaces are more frequent. Poplar forest spreads about in clumps, dotting here and there among the stretches of hilly grassland. Andrei sees more of the river, and soon the silver glint of the Batoche church steeple rises behind a cover of trees. A bell rings.

"Marie Alberta Julianna calls us," Gabriel says.

"Marie?" Andrei asks.

"The church bell. There used to be another one. Marie Antoinette."

Marie smiles. "Why two? And why both named *Marie?*"

"The English stole the first one. There was some fighting and the English took Marie Antoinette from the church." He points toward the river to the white crosses of a graveyard.

"Many were killed in the fighting. You will see bullet holes in the church. I was three years old and I remember Uncle Moise coming home, his shoulder bleeding from the gunshot."

Andrei stares back to the crosses.

Carriages and two-wheeled carts pulled by horses and oxen fall in from three directions heading for the church. Teams are tied in the shade of trees and people funnel into the church. Andrei can see the bullet holes on the wall. People assemble together in crowds along this wall, and out front. A man in a black suit and black leather boots waves to Gabriel from the steps.

"That's Uncle Moise," Gabriel says. "He's found room for us inside."

"He doesn't look the same," Andrei says.

"Dressed up for church," Gabriel says.

The pews are packed with people. Moise leads Gabriel, Marie, and Andrei in a line, close to the front. He points with his good arm, flicking the fingers of his hand, and three boys Andrei's age, one of them Chi Pete, step over legs and squeeze themselves forward out of the pew into the aisle. Chi Pete shrugs his shoulders and waves, then bumps into the black iron stove as wide as a coffin sitting five feet from the communion rail. Its pipe rises ten feet straight up, bends to the middle of the church, then rises again, straight up through the roof. The uncle whispers in Chi Pete's ear, then pulls him by the shoulder out the door.

Andrei glances at Gabriel.

"You'll catch up with him later this afternoon," Gabriel

says. "At the fairgrounds. Right now he has to help with the Procession."

The mass lasts for two hours. On the way to Batoche, Gabriel had said that everything but the sermon would be in Latin. The sermon would be French. He said that they wouldn't want to hear Father Moulin anyway. All he ever preached about were the evils of liquor, dancing, fiddle playing, cards, and pool.

Many things are familiar to Andrei. Holy pictures adorn the walls. Candles burn on the altar. The priest dresses in a golden robe and he makes the sign of the cross, maybe not always repeated three times in a row like Ukrainians do, but still it's the sign of the cross. What is most familiar is the incense. The priest carries the brass burner on a chain, and he swings it every chance he gets.

He parts the golden curtains on the centre of the altar. Out of the tabernacle comes a golden cup. He lifts a white wafer out of the cup and holds it in his fingers above his head. He lays it on a silver plate and three times swings the incense burner. He walks to a side table and comes back holding a brass sunburst. He opens the small, round glass door at the centre of the sunburst, placing the wafer inside. He sets it on the altar and again wafts incense, from the left, the front, and from the right.

Uncle Moise comes to the front holding a silver crucifix mounted on a five-foot pole supported on a belt around his waist.

"In spite of his bad arm," Gabriel whispers, "Uncle Moise will play the fiddle tonight. After all these years, he's got some feeling back in three of his fingers, though he still can't lift the bad arm above his head."

Another man follows Moise, carrying the banner of St. Joseph. Four boys, including Chi Pete, stand ready with lighted candles. Finally they are going outside to the fresh air.

The people flowing out of the church join the throngs outside, all of them following the crucifix. Women carry rosaries and Andrei hears the hushed rumble of French prayers. Gabriel has said that his people pray in French and hunt in Cree.

Though it's not Ukrainian, the procession seems to warm Andrei, seems to fill him with a sense of well-being. The walk of the people reminds him of his lost homeland, with its colours, and the smell of incense and candles burning... Andrei belonging in the pageantry. Uncle Moise holds the silver crucifix high, leading them in the direction of the river, to an outdoor altar where the people kneel and pray. After long minutes, Uncle Moise rises, and he leads the procession back to the church, as the people sing, and pray the rosary.

The priest stands at the altar, facing the people. They are kneeling in their pews. He raises the sunburst in his blessing. He then sets it down, takes the wafer from its centre, and places it in the chalice. He parts the golden curtains and returns the Holy Sacrament back to its safety in the tabernacle.

GABRIEL DRIVES THE BUGGY along the trail following the river to the Village of Batoche, half a mile northwest of the church. To their right are the fairgrounds, a wide open stretch of prairie rising to a broad hillside in the east.

"La Belle Prairie," Gabriel says. *"La Jolie Prairie."*

The grounds soon cover with crowds. Women stand chatting in groups, some in white dresses and bonnets, others in black done up snugly with long rows of tiny buttons. Some carry parasols blotting out the sun. Men in groups wear black suits and felt hats. Several in a line hold bulls on leads. One man with a tall top hat balances on a bicycle with a tiny back wheel and a front wheel five feet high. Gypsies cart goods out of three red-and-gold circus wagons. They've set up booths and a fortune teller's tent.

Gabriel stops in front of a bluff at the top of the steep-sloped riverbank. He unhitches Raven and ties the horse to a tree. Gabriel's going to race him. He wants Andrei to brush him down, then let him rest in the shade. They won't be racing until later in the afternoon.

"Let's spread a blanket here," Gabriel says. "It's in the shade and out of the way. I'll be busy with the races, and it's getting hotter and hotter. Some of the time in the afternoon, you might want to get away from the crowds. It's just perfect for that right here."

They've parked the buggy between the bluff and a magnificent house. A rail fence surrounds it, some of it collapsed, some still standing. The house has board siding painted white with blue trim. The many windows have louvred shutters, some sagging, some of them gone.

"This was Mr. Letendre's house," Gabriel says. "He still owns the store, but he doesn't live here anymore. He rents the store to an Englishman from Duck Lake. Mr. Letendre sold the house to the police for a barracks, and he bought a ranch maybe ten miles south of your homestead."

A veranda surrounds two sides of the house, supported every six feet with latticed posts. A round window looks out from the face of a third-storey centre-gabled roof. A cupola rises from the very top of the house.

"What's it for?" Andrei asks.

"A ventilator," Gabriel says. "That's some house, eh? I wanted to show it to the both of you. I want you to know something more about my people. Something more than what you might hear."

At the fairgrounds, people stare, but more at Marie than Andrei, and their dark eyes are friendly. The colour of Marie's attire stands out, as the women's dresses are either white or black. But some of their blouses are bright with beadwork, and some with embroidered flowers. A girl Andrei's age wears a black dress with matching stockings. Her hair is done in a braid tied with a white ribbon jutting below the rim of her broad-brimmed hat.

In the entry to a tent, a Gypsy woman waves to Andrei.

"Go ahead," Gabriel says. "She wants to tell your fortune...for a price, of course," and he hands Andrei a dime.

Should he go? The woman keeps waving, her bracelets jangling on her wrists.

"Ask my fortune," Marie says.

"Ask her yourself."

"I wouldn't dare," Marie says, grinning at Gabriel.

Every year after the harvest, Gypsies had camped by Andrei's village, and often people went to have their fortunes told. Andrei will go in, just to see what a fortune teller does.

She closes the tent flap. Inside on a small table covered with red velvet, sits a glass ball. Beside it, smoke curls up from a brass burner, filling the tent with the heavy scent of incense. A monkey sits tied to a stake in a far corner. The woman's long fingers tuck the tresses of her hair inside her black-and-red silk shawl. Her fingers lower from her face to hover around the ball. She hums and nods for several moments.

"You want something very badly," she says. "Yes, very badly, and you are searching for ways to get it."

How does she know that, Andrei wonders?

"You will work hard to save money." For a long time she stares, squinting, drawing back her head as if trying to pull out a picture. "I can't quite see..."

"Is it a horse?" Andrei asks.

"Wait...yes. Yes, a horse, a beautiful horse..."

"Is it a bay?"

"Red...yes, a bay horse with a boy riding, galloping across a meadow...a church...they follow a path to where it pairs off...one of the paths to good, and the other to evil.... Oh! Something bright..."

"Like the sun bursting...? A gold sun on a stand with a glass centre...?"

"Yes...gold."

"A cup of gold?"

"Yes, gold. The brightness of gold...it's fading, fading." She caresses the ball with her fingers. She rubs it, staring with her dark eyes, blinking. "Nothing more...I see nothing. The gold has turned all white. In all directions, nothing but cold white!" She stares again, wipes her eyes, blinks, blinks, and stares, all at once whipping back her head. "No! No!" she says. "No, it's nothing. Nothing more."

She turns away from the ball. "Perhaps if you pay another dime..."

Andrei hasn't any money. What he earns at Kuzyk's, he's saving for the colt. Mr. Kuzyk hasn't said how much he wants for the colt. What if it's a hundred dollars? He could never earn that much. So what difference would ten cents make? He could ask Gabriel, but he won't. Gabriel has been too good to him for Andrei to ask more favours, and he doesn't put much store in this fortune teller's skills. She hasn't told him anything that he doesn't already know. Andrei's secret is at the rock. Surely Dido will go back there, and Andrei will go with him. She didn't mention the Scythian guards. Perhaps at the rock the warriors will appear, as they did in his vision of the cave, and this time they might tell him wonderful things.

From their picnic blanket, Andrei gazes out at the crowds of people. He can't find Chi Pete.

"He must have gone home after church," Gabriel says. "Don't worry. He'll show up. Let's have our lunch."

Gabriel has bought meat pies, and a bread pudding on which he pours syrup he says is made from the sap of birch trees. He's brought oranges, and he hands one to Andrei.

"What is it?" Andrei asks.

"Fruit. Go ahead. Eat it."

"What kind of fruit?"

"An orange. They sell them at the store. Go ahead. Eat it."

He bites into the hard skin, chews, then squints at Gabriel.

"You have to peel it first," Marie says, as if she knew that all along. He squeezes the orange instead, the juice suddenly sweet in his mouth. He tears it in half and sinks his teeth into the flesh, tearing it from the peel. He's never tasted anything so deliciously sweet and tart all at the same time. When he's done, he watches as Marie still plays with hers. She breaks the orange into segments, placing a portion on her tongue, all the while her eyes on Gabriel across the blanket from her. She chews, licking her lips, and her eyes sparkle.

After they finish their lunch, Marie stays at the blanket. Gabriel takes Andrei to a group of nine boys assembled on the racetrack.

"There's Chi Pete," Andrei says. Two men hold a length of string at the finish line. The boys eye Andrei; some are laughing.

"*Chi,*" one of them says, pointing at Andrei. "*Chi! Chi!*"

"Don't let them bother you," Chi Pete says.

"He's calling me your name," Andrei says.

"It's nothing," Chi Pete says. "*Chi* means 'little,' that's all." He shakes Andrei's hand, then gestures by swatting the air in the direction of the rude companions. Andrei should pay no attention to them.

As they line up, Andrei takes off his shoes. He's one of the younger boys; some of them are thirteen, some fourteen, the taller boys all arms and legs.

The gun fires. He's off like a rabbit and doesn't look back. He glances over his shoulder just once and sees that he's in the lead. Just ahead is the string stretched across the track. He wins...he breaks through the string.

Andrei bends forward, hands on his knees, gulping air. A judge pats him on the back and gives him his prize of twenty-five cents. The boys gather around him, laughing again, but not at his expense. This time they shake their heads and pat him on the back. Several boys flex their arms, bulging their biceps.

Chi Pete points to a crowd of people gathering in a circle. The next competition is the arm wrestle. Each boy tests his strength against another. Through a process of elimination a winner is found and it's not Andrei. But he comes close. He's third in their group of ten. All of the digging and haying and pulling of roots at the farm has toughened him.

"Vite, vite," Chi Pete says. He grabs Andrei's hand, then lets go and points to the crowd gathering further up the track.

Horses jostle at the starting line. Fifteen riders, some of them tugging at reins, others patting their horses' necks, try to form in line. Others spin in circles, some rearing up.

When it appears the line-up is as good as it will get, the starter fires his pistol, and the twirling pack of horses whips apart in a flurry of dust and pounding hooves. Three horses fail to make the first turn, hurling in a straight line off the track through a fleeing crowd of spectators. Andrei can see across the oval where three horses are out front, with Raven ten lengths behind running in the middle of the pack. As they come into the turn, he finds some room and breaks away. Coming down the stretch he's running third, five lengths behind the second horse.

Raven is a big horse with long legs and a massive chest built for endurance. Into the backstretch of the second lap, he's running second and gaining on the leader. On the turn, the rider on the lead horse looks back over his shoulder. Raven's right on his tail and the rider whips his horse again and again. Gabriel leans forward, his head alongside Raven's neck. They keep this pace around the turn. Once on the home stretch, the big horse seems to swell out his chest, his legs stretching further and further, making it seem as if Raven's black body flies through the air. He leaps into the lead...one length, two, three. He's out front by five lengths at the finish line.

There is one more special event before the killing of the ox. Three riders, including Gabriel, remain on the track. They form up in place at the north end of the home stretch. At the sound of the gun they are off. Nearing the crowd, each rider stands on his head, moccasins pointed to the sky, each horse at full gallop.

From the south they return. Two riders vault from their saddles, feet touching the ground, then swinging back up on their horses. Gabriel does a double vault. He swings down on the right side, shoots back up and over to the other side, and then back again, mounted upright on Raven.

Finally, old Uncle Moise places three cloths on the track; red, yellow, and green. Gabriel has told Andrei that, in the days of the buffalo hunts, each rider marked the animal he downed, not stopping as he dropped a coloured rag by its side, but instead racing off to shoot another buffalo.

The three riders race again from the north, each to retrieve his cloth. Each bends far to the side, head low to the ground. Each grabs his cloth from the track. Andrei can't be certain how Gabriel does it, but as he swings back up on Raven, the red cloth is not in Gabriel's hand, but, as if he's a Cossack, Gabriel has the prize gripped in his teeth.

At four o'clock the ox to be killed stands free in the middle of the field, but it seems out of place, head swaying back and forth, confused and alone. Hundreds of people rim the perimeter of the track, all of them ready to watch. Métis horsemen pose stripped to the waist, trotting their horses on to the field. Each man holds a strung bow and an arrow. All at once they speed around and around in a circle. They draw their bows, each man in turn leaning to the ox, shooting his arrow. A rider leaps from his horse, grabbing the ox by the horns and stabbing it in the throat. Blood streams to the ground, jetting in spurts to the beat of the brute's heart. It wavers on its feet, then stumbles, the front legs buckling, the body tumbling to the ground. The animal's limbs jut in frantic jerks in its final dance of death.

A group of women enter the oval. They lay the ox stretched out on its back, to butcher it the way Gabriel did the moose, preparing for roasting on hot coals.

In the evening in the centre of the oval, a bonfire burns. Uncle Moise plays the violin with three other fiddlers, and an accordion plays. Young people dance. Men talk in groups around the fire, drinking wine or homemade whiskey. Women tend to the roasting meat. When it is ready, each person will have a taste. Gabriel says this was the way it was done during the time of the buffalo hunts.

THE POPLAR FOREST seems more alive at night. Though Andrei sees nothing in the blackness, the moonlight casts a glaze on the cutline of the wagon trail. He imagines eyes of yellow and green glowing from somewhere deep in the blackness. An owl hoots. Coyote pups yip and yap over a midnight supper. A wolf howls an unknown sadness, something ancient and alone. Trees could well have arms with spindly fingers, knot-holes turned to eyes and jagged mouths. A sudden breath of a wind shakes leaves as if the trees walk in their rustle of forest dress. Above, the stars of the Milky Way appear to race in a swirl of spirits.

The trail passes along the rim of a coulee. Andrei hears frogs croaking somewhere down at the water below. Raven jerks at his harness, and he snorts, picking up speed.

"Whoa, easy boy," Gabriel says with a pull on the lines.

"What is it?" Marie asks. She slides closer to Gabriel, clutching his shoulder and peering to the side into the darkness.

Andrei fidgets in the back of the buggy, like the Gypsy's monkey in the tent. The skin on his face tightens, the twitch he can't control. He's spinning in the air, flung high into the secret rainbow world where he's overcome and drawn to visions. Rainbow colours pulse in waves throughout the darkness, and down the hill, from the giant rock, from out of its crevices, from out of the rock animal's mouth, gold strings leak like spider legs. A red spot shines from the face of the rock. From Raven's nostrils tongues of fire shoot, the flames tumbling down the hillside, where they mingle with the strings, and snap like lightning. Sparks fly into the air...sparks turned to horses, like stars across the sky.

A shadow forms atop the rock, shaking a rattle. Andrei floats above the wagon, twirling head over heels in the swirling rainbow clouds. Finally something strikes him, pulls at him.

"Andrei! Andrei!" Strong hands grip his shoulders, shaking him. "Settle down, Andrei." Gabriel shakes him again. "Were you having a nightmare? You must have been sleeping." Gabriel sits him down in the back of the buggy.

"Where are we?" Andrei asks.

"On the trail," Gabriel says. "Something spooked Raven. Maybe a lynx in the trees. Or a bear. Maybe you spooked him. You were standing up and yelling, 'Skomar! Snow Walker! Skomar! Snow Walker!'"

"You didn't see him?"

"Who?"

"Snow Walker. On top of the rock."

"You must have been dreaming," Gabriel says.

"Let's get out of here," Marie says.

"Maybe Snow Walker is out there," Gabriel says. "You never know with him." He lights his pipe and flicks gently with the reins. "You've had these dreams before, Andrei?"

"Maybe sometimes," Andrei says. "Something like that." He doesn't want to say anything more. He should talk to Dido.

Somewhere ahead of them, the Baydas' shelter hunches in

its moonlit clearing, waiting for the morning, and waiting for the late night return of Andrei and Marie. Andrei wonders about the cup. Something was out of sorts down there at the rock. Dido should never have buried the cup there. It is not the place for Scythian warriors.

CHAPTER 11

Andrei has hardly fallen asleep before Tato is waking him.

"Neighbours come," he says, pushing at Andrei's shoulder. "Hurry! You want them to catch you still in bed? Some boys your age are already here."

Several men and women congregate in front of the *buda.* They have come to build the new house. Mr. Kuzyk has brought people from as far as Alvena, seven miles away. Three boys about Andrei's age have each climbed a tree, and they caw at each other like crows.

"Get down!" a man says. "At once! I brought you to work. You want to play with trees, there will be enough limbs for you to cut."

The boys run off with Andrei to examine Kuzyk's team of bay mares. He has hauled in a wagonload of logs already squared. With the ones the family has already prepared, they'll have enough to build a finished house. And Mr. Kuzyk is an expert carpenter. Everybody knows that Mr. Kuzyk was head carpenter in the building of the church.

"This mare has a colt at home," Andrei says. "I'm going to buy him when I earn enough money."

"What's your name?" one of the boys asks.

"I'm Andrei Bayda, Cossack." It's not a lie. Sometimes Dido calls him *Cossack.*

"We're Smuks," another says.

"I'm Robbin."

"I'm Bobbin."

"I'm Dobbin."

They say this on the run, as if they've practiced, twirling in a circle around Andrei.

"What kind of names are those?" They keep circling. Their mother must have placed a bowl on their heads to cut their hair. Each haircut is the same, a ball cut in half above the ears. Each boy looks the same, button nose, bare feet, baggy trousers cut off at the knees.

"Horses' names," one boy says.

"Our dad was a groom in the army," another says.

"What army?" Andrei asks. "Cossacks?"

"The Austrian army," the second boy says.

"Was he in the cavalry?" Andrei asks.

"He was a groom," the third boy says. "A groom brushes horses. Our dad knows horses."

"Andrei!" someone yells from the yard.

"We better go see what they want us to do," Andrei says. "Let's race." They take off in a scramble, but Andrei wins without even having to run that hard.

THE BUSH RINGS with the chopping of trees. The boys are everywhere trimming branches, and men drag and carry trees to the yard. Wood chips fly from broadaxes squaring the logs. Tato waves to a man with an ox dragging a stoneboat. They lift off rocks and lay them flat at four corners. A first row of logs forms the rectangle of the house.

Mr. Kuzyk dovetails the ends of the logs. Another man drills with an auger and pounds wooden pegs into the holes. The walls rise one row of logs at a time. The neighbours come five days in a row, taking time away from their own work. Thank goodness most of the haying is done in the district, and the wheat is not quite ripe enough yet to cut and stook. "God finds us time," Mama says.

"Cut willows," Tato tells the boys.

Saplings for laths run diagonally up the walls, inside and out. The boys tramp bare feet in the clay pit. Marie carries buckets from the well and pours water into the pit. A roof beam supports log rafters leaning up to it. Poles are laid side by side, crosswise, for the ceiling. Tato and Mr. Kuzyk, at opposite ends of a saw, cut out a doorway and three window openings. Buckets and shovels full of clay are carried from the pit, and women plaster the inside walls and ceiling. Others start on the outside. Tall grass is bundled and carried up on ladders to the roof.

Every day Mama makes soup with early potatoes, onions, and beet greens from the garden, and she stirs it in a huge black pot set on the iron ring over the cooking fire. People have to eat, and those who came from far stay here all five days and sleep under the spruce trees.

On the fifth day at dusk the job is finished. A perfect house. The entrance faces south, opening to a storeroom in the middle of the building. To the left is the kitchen and sleeping room. To the right the special room faces east. It's here where the Holy pictures will be hung, where meals will be served on Holy Days, the room used when visitors come. Mama will finish building the clay oven in the kitchen and sleeping room. Tato says that after harvest he will buy a proper iron heater for the east room. The house smells of new wood and the clean and tangy smell of lime and wet clay.

The workers collect as a group, facing the house. Andrei's off to the side with the Smuk boys watching. Mama and Tato stand in the doorway sheltered under the full width of the thatch overhang. Mr. Kuzyk's cantor voice leads in a peoples' blessing that has for centuries stirred the Ukrainian soul. *May you live many, many years. For your health and your blessing, may you live many, many, years.* Mr. Kuzyk stands out as solemn and dignified as a priest. Over and over Andrei hears his bass voice leading in the singing of the refrain: *May you live many many years.* Mama goes to her knees, and three times crosses herself. She wipes her eyes with a corner of her apron. Tato also prays on his knees. The tears fall from their faces. Everyone prays. *Our Father, who art in Heaven...*

THE NEXT MORNING Dido ties Frank to a tree in order to trim his hooves. Andrei sits on a stump watching.

Dido swings his arm through the air and the horse flinches. "Hand me the rasp, Andrei. Easy, easy," he says to the horse, patting his flank in the process of lifting a back foot. Andrei leans forward, reaching out with the rasp, his other hand shielding his head.

"You think he will kick?" Dido says. "Not Frank. He likes me, and maybe he's also too lazy to kick." He trims with a knife, then files back and forth on the hoof. "Hetman Bayda raised the world's finest horses. He raced them over the steppes."

"What is a Hetman?"

"The head man," Dido says. "Your ancestor Bayda-Vyshnevetsky!"

"Did you know Hetman Bayda?"

"Not exactly. It was three hundred years ago when he ruled."

Dido Danylo sits on the ground and packs tobacco into his long-stemmed pipe. He lights it and Andrei smells the sweet aroma.

"Did you have a sabre like the Hetman Bayda?"

"Not exactly." Dido Danylo stands up. He leads the horse to the well and draws water to pour into the rough plank trough. "But if I had lived three hundred years ago, I would have had a sabre."

When Frank drinks his fill, Dido stands on the well and climbs up on the horse.

"Get on," he says to Andrei. Dido makes a clicking sound with his tongue, but the horse doesn't move. He jabs his heels at Frank's ribs and slaps the leather lines on his rump. Frank breaks into a walk.

The morning started with a clear blue sky, and with Dido

playing a merry tune of the Hetman Bayda on his flute. But now black clouds rumble in the west, and Dido no longer brags of Cossacks. The air is absolutely still, the only sound a faint rumble of thunder. Dido doesn't say a word, doesn't look around, only straight ahead as if he knows exactly where he's going. His silence is out of the ordinary for Dido. Usually he would have brought along his flute. He should be sitting up proudly on Frank playing the song of Hetman Bayda. Today instead, something wears on Dido's mind. Andrei guesses that Dido is taking him to the rock. He should have told Dido about Snow Walker.

"I WAS NOT TO TELL A SOUL," Dido says. "But I can now that we are finally settled. You must be shown, Andrei. The Holy one told me that perils and destruction were coming to the lands of Ukraine. He said that some of the people should leave, that I, Danylo Skomar, with my grandson, Andrei, should take the goatskin bag and leave. What can be more homely than goatskin? But what golden secrets does it have inside? The Holy one vowed that in the bag are the keys to the future. You acted strangely when you saw the cup."

"It showed me its golden halo," Andrei says. "I believe it wants to take me places."

"Who knows what it can or cannot do?" Dido says. "The Holy one told of our Skomar ancestor and a Gypsy fortune teller...in the same breath as pledging homage to the Hetman Bayda-Vyshnevetsky." Dido leans over on the horse and spits on the ground. Under his breath he mumbles, "Maybe it is

Uncle Skomar who tempts us all the way from Ukraine." He turns his head around and stares at Andrei. Dido's eyes seem far away, and his topknot hangs over the corner of his mouth, as if he's disturbed in his thoughts.

Andrei sees the large rock jutting up from out of its depression in the hillside. They dismount and, Dido leading the horse, the boy and his grandfather walk down the hill.

"I'm an old man already," Dido says, and he swats a mosquito full of blood, leaving a red stain on his forehead.

Andrei hasn't heard Dido talk like this before. Usually he's singing of some merry new adventure. Today it's like he's planning his own funeral.

"Old like Frank." Dido stops walking and hands the reins to Andrei. His long braid lifts, with his hand shading his brow as he looks in every direction. Three or four crows fly from one clump of trees to another. The clouds churn overhead.

"We will see what it shows us," Dido says.

"Maybe it can tell us the future."

"Yes. Yes. I don't want to go to my grave without knowing."

"You're not ready to go to the grave yet, Dido."

The overcast sky blots out the sun. Far to the west, lightning flashes. The air is thick and heavy, with an added tinge of the smell of sulphur.

"Everybody goes to the grave," Dido says. "Some before others. Usually the old before the young. Me before you, Andrei. The Holy man directed that we pass the secrets of the past, the secrets of the old world, to the new generation in the new world. You are the new generation, Andrei. Yet I wish to know before I die."

Why doesn't Dido tell this to Tato? Does Andrei want the responsibility of carrying the Holy fool's magic? It's here on this hillside, the place on their way back from Batoche where he saw the golden fire in tangles snaking from the rock's mouth, back and forth with the fire from Raven's nose. Fire changed to horses in the sky when he saw Snow Walker standing on the broad hump of the rock's shoulders.

"What has it shown you already, Dido? What did the cup tell you that day at the homestead?"

"Nothing," Dido says. "Remember at the Cossack burial mound? The Holy man took me away? He said to take the charm to safety, that it may guide our people in the new world, that it may bring riches."

"Is it safe here?"

"It seems almost a sacred place," Dido says.

"Where is it buried?" Andrei descends into the depression to the rock's face. He stares at the head, the mouth, the crack where he found the brass button. He walks behind the rock and watches, Dido on his knees, digging at the base of the rock.

"Don't go on your knees, Dido."

"What are you saying? How else am I to dig?"

With his knife he lifts up the sod. At ground level the rock is layered with cracks. Dido pulls pieces of shale from the rock, from down and in, many pieces, as if from a puzzle. Then he reaches, groping for the bag inside. He pulls it out and places it on the rock, draws out the lacquered box with its stars and crescent moons carved into the wood.

"Inside is the secret," Dido says. He takes on the appearance of a boy whispering to a boy. Instead of the sound of a grandfather's wise counsel, Dido's voice quavers with awe. He and Andrei are about to witness the unknown, and Dido's age counts for nothing.

"The Holy fool told me," Dido says, "that the talisman fascinates anyone who beholds it. The very limits of human thought, it contains. It knows the intimate secrets of men and women. It captures souls. Yet he warned that the cup can sometimes give you back only your own thoughts, only your own dreams and nightmares, that you imagine predict the future." As Dido says these words, he peers every which way, eyes like buttons shutting secrets away from intruders.

Andrei doesn't want Dido to open the box. Can it be that once the secret is out it can't be put back in? That it will fly away with the crows? Dido lifts the brass clasp and opens the lid. He takes out the cup wrapped in black cloth and sets it on the ground, opening the wrap.

Frank neighs and paws at the ground, his ears flat against his head, stepping back, his reins dragging in the grass.

An explosion of light forks down from the sky, claps of thunder shaking the ground. Then all around the landscape darkens. Water droplets splatter. Andrei's attention is drawn to the cup on the black cloth. The ruby pulses with the pulling force of a magnet. The muscles in Andrei's neck tighten. His eyes water and burn. It's as if the stars in the sky tumble into a cavity the size of the ocean, funnelling deep into its depths, a pulsing swirl of the halo and the circle of the heads of horses.

The longer Andrei stares, the more his head swims. A forest grows in this universe, images coming together in the cup. The visions appear to him as clear and real as a boy's dream, where anything is possible, everything believed. He sees a thick clump of willows. Ghosts weave through the branches, parts of bodies, a patch here and a patch there, like a puzzle, separating and coming together. The horses race around the rim. The mounted Cossacks on the grassy meadow. The dancing girls in a circle. His old dog Brovko howls, "Come back home, Andrei."

The dream continues, on and on, in splashes of warm colours and comfort, a world as Andrei would wish it, and as tantalizing as a fairy tale with pots of gold. Are the riders Cossacks racing at Batoche? A Gypsy woman sits in the entry of her tent beckoning for Andrei to have his fortune told. The horses gallop in the vision...those of the cup, or are they Kuzyk's? Yet in the vision, Gabriel rides black Raven, the horse leaping and fire blazing from his nostrils.

All at once Andrei's sense of well-being in his sleep-world disappears. The horse Frank stumbles riderless, yellow eyes staring through straggles of hair. But Kuzyk's bay colt races. Petrus Shumka dances a wedding dance. Andrei's temple throbs as he flies twirling in his rainbow world.

Andrei doesn't remember returning home, but he does remember bits and pieces of his visions. On the one hand he saw riches, yet on the other, his path is strewn with dangers. When he questions Dido, all that his grandfather will tell him is that he passed out in a fit. To get Andrei home, Dido had to lift him, and lay him like a sack of oats across the horse's back.

August

CHAPTER 12

THIS MORNING BEFORE THE MOSQUITOES GOT TOO BAD, Mr. Kuzyk, his mother, Andrei's mother, and Marie picked chokecherries. By nine o'clock Mr. Kuzyk's mother insisted that Mama and Marie join them on a trip to Rosthern, to help choose a new suit for Mr. Kuzyk. Tato and Dido have gone again to the Klassen farm, and Andrei's alone where Mr. Kuzyk's left him to plough a field. He wants to earn enough money to buy the colt, but it may take more than this summer's work. Mr. Kuzyk says that horses are very expensive in Canada, just like in the Old Country. The colt is from a fine line of horses. Its mother is Mr. Kuzyk's pet. If he weren't training a pair of two-year-olds for the buggy, he would have taken his favourite, the bay mare, to Rosthern today.

Andrei's driving Mr. Kuzyk's heavy horse team. The lines are tied, draped over his left shoulder, down across his back and looped around under his right arm. Both his hands are free to cling to the handles of the walking plough. Mosquitoes swarm around his head as he stumbles over the furrow. It seems almost a relief when one of the horses lifts its tail and releases droppings, as if the aroma kills mosquitoes. The plough snags on a root, the horses straining, jerking; and finally the root's cut through. Relief comes only at every smouldering brush pile, the horses then reluctant to leave the smoke. Andrei urges them forward, and the hum of mosquitoes further drives the team onward to the next pile.

Mr. Kuzyk chopped the trees out two winters ago. He pulled the stumps in the spring and stacked them in piles. Early this morning, he set them on fire. This afternoon a flame flickers only now and then, but the smoke rises in a steady drift.

By late afternoon, when the mosquitoes are at their worst, the horses refuse to leave the smoke. Andrei wears trousers of coarse fabric, a shirt of Old Country heavy linen snug at his wrists and neck. Around his head he's tied a scarf. The clothing's soaked from his labours in the early August heat, but his discomfort concentrates only on mosquitoes. Mr. Kuzyk says it should be too late in the year for mosquitoes, but July has been hot and the bush seems always damp. He says that only a frost will finish them off, and that won't be for at least another month. So far the nights have stayed warm.

Today Andrei can work no longer, and that's fine because the horses won't either. He unhitches the team. They're willing to move now, sensing that Andrei will drive them to the creek and a drink, and from there to the shelter of the barn.

All Andrei hears is a snorting. He knows that the colt and

its mother are pastured in the meadow where Mr. Kuzyk has finished the haying. The creek borders the south end of the meadow where the grass peters out, and the ground is sour, caked white where nothing grows. He hears more snorting. Far ahead he sees the colt running in small circles. It's only then that Andrei spots the mare.

She's bogged in a soap hole of slippery white mud. The mosquitoes are less abundant here; the sour smell of the salty muck must keep them away. But it must have attracted the mare. She's sunk down past her knees. The more she squirms, the more her rump sinks down. Her head tosses, eyes white. Ears back. Her body is caked with the mud. She must have been rolling in it, crazy from mosquitoes. The colt flits nervously from one side of her to the other, edging closer into the muck, then backing away.

Andrei wishes Gabriel were here; he'd know what to do. Or Dido. But neither are here, so it's no use to wish. He has the team. Thank goodness he's had the full day to practice. He knows how to turn the horses, how to back them, keep them from running away, but if they decided to run, how could he ever stop them? Do the horses let him handle them because they know he likes horses? He has to try and pull the mare out of the bog with the team.

A rope is coiled around the hames of one of the horses.

"Easy, girl. Easy." He shouldn't have to worry; she won't be going anywhere the way she is now. He pats the mare on her neck, working his way with his hands along her back. He tries to step lightly in the muck so as not to sink himself. Mr. Kuzyk would sink for sure. He shoves down in the mud with

the rope, trying to force it through under the mare's belly. He thinks he should pull her from the rear. The pull might be too hard on her neck. It might choke her, or a sudden jerk might break her neck. But try as he might, the mare's hind quarters are sunk too far in. He can't get the rope around her. He tries around her chest just behind the front legs, and even there she's sunk too deep. She'll have to be pulled from the neck.

But first he has to do something about the front feet. He looks about in the shrubs and finds a stout stick for digging in the mud. He breaks up clumps, lifting the wet muck out with his hands. He digs a hole all the way down to the mare's front hooves. He finds more sticks and lays them in the hole, keeping the hooves free.

The colt stands off ten feet away. If Andrei didn't know better, he'd say that it knows the mare's in trouble, and that Andrei's trying to help. He secures the rope around the neck. The mare snorts and waves her head sideways and up and down. Andrei lays the rope out and goes for the team.

"Easy, boys, easy." The geldings stand, leaning forward in the harness, the rope tight. "Easy. Easy." Andrei's right by the mare's head, the lines in his hands. He flicks them lightly. The horses pull.

The noose tightens and tightens around the mare's neck. Andrei senses a sudden frenzy, both in himself, and in the mare; it seems that the whites of her eyes will shoot out of her head. The mare's choking. Andrei backs the team. As quick as he can, he's at the noose, prying it open with his fingers.

He needs something else to tie to the mare. Mr. Kuzyk's

stump-pulling chain is where he left it at the edge of the breaking, wrapped around the arm of a tree. Andrei leads the team to a spot by the creek away from the soap hole, where he ties halter shanks to willow shrubs, then runs non-stop for the chain. He runs as fast as he did in the races at Batoche, and five times as far, fast even on the way back dragging a chain.

With the chain fastened around the mare's neck, hooked so that it can tighten no more, the horses pull again. The mare's shoulders twitch and roll, her head and neck twisting under the strain. The hooves scramble in the sticks. A front foot plunges into the muck. The horse snorts and the foot springs back out with a smack of a sucking sound. The team steady in its pull. Snorts and sucks. Snorts and sucks. The colt flits again, back and forth, watching, ears laid back.

"Haahhh!" A yell comes, cursing in the name of diseases, *"Cholera!"* Shouts from a distance, *"Cholera! Cholera!"* Mr. Kuzyk swears in the Ukrainian practice of naming diseases. *"Cholera!* What are you doing with my horse?"

His bulk tumbles over the meadow, half running, half walking, all out of breath. He gets to the bog just as the mare's emerging, free at last. Andrei hands the lines to Mr. Kuzyk then fall to his knees, sobbing uncontrollably.

CHAPTER 13

IT HAS BECOME ROUTINE FOR MR. KUZYK'S BUGGY AND BAY mare to suddenly appear at Bayda's, but this visit is different. And it's not only because he's left the bay at home. This time Mr. Kuzyk seems different.

"The mare must have been stuck in that bog all night and day," he says to Andrei, who stands at the front of the team, gripping the bridle on one of the jittery two-year-olds. "I spent an hour rubbing her down, but she got a terrible chill. I think she'll survive, but she's not well. Getting her back to health will take time."

He doesn't peer over Andrei's head to the garden, nor to the well. Doesn't glance to the side as if expecting Marie to be standing in the doorway of the house. This time his attention's glued to Andrei. He doesn't cringe, doesn't cover his mouth and cough. His head doesn't scrunch down into the fleshy folds of his neck. His eyes don't squint and waver. He sits tall in the buggy, taller than he really is, or at least taller than Andrei remembers.

"But all in all, she'll be fine."

"Does she have milk for the colt?" Andrei asks.

"That's what I want to see you about. The colt has to be weaned. There's no milk, and even if there was, feeding the colt would sap what strength she has. I told you that a colt with his bloodlines is worth a lot of money, and I hoped to keep him as a sire."

Andrei has never given up hope, but he's also been realistic. He's realized that the colt would more than likely be fully grown before he'd even come close to owning it.

"If you want him weaned, won't he have to be kept away from her?"

"That's just it," Mr. Kuzyk says, stepping down from the buggy. He stands face to face with Andrei. At this moment it appears they each have grown in stature. They are about to seal a transaction.

"I think you've come a long way in your quest to own the colt, my boy."

Andrei nods his head. Mr. Kuzyk extends his hand to shake some kind of agreement.

"You can come stook for a week or two," Mr. Kuzyk says. "I have the mare penned. The colt runs loose in the yard. He doesn't go far. In the evenings you can work with the colt. Teach him to lead. Teach him to follow you home. I've decided that after a week or two, you can keep him here to train. Of course he still is mine. He's worth a lot of money, and you know how tough it is to make a living on the farm. But I tell you what. I'll let you take the honour to name him, and if you work enough hours for me by next year's harvest, you just might save enough money to buy him outright."

Andrei has been thinking all summer about a name, and wondering how he could bring up the subject. Now he has the opportunity.

"I know a name already," Andrei says.

"Oh? Well then, why not give it to him right this minute?"

"He will run like the wind," Andrei says. "That's what I name him... *Vityr!*"

"An excellent name," Mr. Kuzyk says. "And come to my farm tomorrow morning. I have lots for you to do." He climbs into his buggy and starts out of the yard. At the last minute he stops, and turns his head to Andrei.

"Just one more thing. I know how hard you can work. But remember that to grow, you also need rest. So," Mr. Kuzyk says, "on the best of days no more work than twelve hours. Understand? That's enough stooking for any man."

STARTING THE NEXT MORNING at Kuzyk's, Andrei works from six o'clock in the morning till six o'clock in the evening. He still has at least three hours of sunlight to train the colt. He carries the halter in one hand and rubs the colt on the neck with the other. The colt steps out of reach and Andrei tries again.

"Good boy, Vityr," he whispers. "Good boy." Andrei moves again slowly, patting the neck, holding out a carrot. Vityr nibbles at it and the carrot falls to the ground. Andrei picks it up and tries again. This time Vityr's lips and teeth hang on, the carrot bobbing, then disappearing into the animal's mouth. Andrei pats again, only this time sliding the halter over Vityr's ears. It hangs loose, but stays on. Andrei continues the rubbing. He rubs the neck on both sides, rubs the ears, and through all this buckles up the halter. "Good boy, Vityr," Andrei says again. He reaches down to rub the belly and the colt runs off.

Every night after supper Andrei's with the colt. By the end of the week he can rub, pat, and caress as much as he wants. Vityr follows him around for more. All Andrei has to do is hold a carrot in his hand and the colt runs to him from across the yard. On Saturday afternoon, Vityr follows Andrei all the way to the Bayda homestead. For the rest of the month, he works with Vityr at home.

September

CHAPTER 14

ANDREI'S DIGGING THE CELLAR HOLE UNDER THE CENTRE storeroom of their house. Mama wants it finished before freeze-up. It's good for potatoes to stay in the ground as long as they can before winter, but they will have to be brought in before it gets too cold.

In this dark and musty hole, Andrei's mind fills with thoughts of the golden cup. He wonders about the visions, and about the big rock on the coulee hillside. About Snow Walker. After Andrei's visit to the rock with Dido, he's been afraid to go back. There are enough dangers in the bush with wolves and bears. He doesn't need the threats of ghosts and shadows, and of spells a Cree medicine man might inflict.

He can think about Vityr. In another year he might be riding him through the forest. It will be at least a year; Vityr has a lot of growing to do yet. But Andrei's already teaching the colt to rein.

Andrei sets the shovel against the cellar wall and climbs

the short ladder, carrying a bucket of dirt. Mama and Marie have gone off into the bush to pick mushrooms. This would be a good time to work with the colt.

The sky's a pale blue with patches of fluffy white clouds, the air filled with garden smells. Brovko dashes across the yard, in pursuit of a rabbit. Andrei digs a carrot from the soil and whistles for the colt. In a flash he's standing at the garden's wattle fence, bobbing his head.

Andrei loops twine through a ring on the halter's chin-strap, then runs each end through makeshift stirrups he's attached to a blanket tied on the colt's back. He walks behind Vityr, holding the ends of the twine, driving the colt across the yard.

"Come here, Brovko," Andrei says. The dog gives a final bark at his vanished rabbit and runs to Andrei's call. They are going for a hike into the bush.

The colt responds to the reins. He can turn right and left. He can stop. He can back up. He can break into a run. By the time winter comes, Andrei wants him to be able to pull a sled.

They trot out of the yard and down the trail, Brovko running ahead, then running back to meet them. He sniffs at trees and follows paths beaten through willow shrubs. Andrei runs the colt. Stops him. They walk. They go on like this all the way to the coulee. He's so busy with Vityr that for the time being he's forgotten about the possibility of spooks and spirits. At the coulee, Andrei pulls the twine out of the stirrups and leads the colt. He decides to explore. There's nothing to be afraid of.

They go down the coulee hill, keeping a distance from the rock, except for Brovko, who runs all over. At the bottom of the coulee, they cross on a deer trail through the willow bluffs and over a dry creek bed. A faint trail follows along the other side of the creek. They take it to where the coulee forks, splitting right and left. They follow to the right, the trail a carpet of green grass where deer have been grazing. Andrei notices small clumps of their droppings, and single pellets spread here and there in the grass. Brovko sniffs the trail. An eroded clay bank looms above them, straight up twenty feet. The clay is streaked in spots with layers of charcoal and white ashes. Further along, the narrow fork widens into a bowl-like plateau. They enter a place with trees spread about, the kind with the twisted trunks and branches, each tree, it seems, reaching in a different direction, all of them bent.

As soon as Andrei spots the cabin, at least a dozen magpies chatter and squawk, as if Andrei's party has invaded their domain. They fly from branch to branch, high and low, crossing paths. They swoop and soar. It would seem they are protecting their nests, but the season is long past hatching time. Most of the birds that swoop and dive are likely this spring's hatch.

They fly here and there...dart off toward the cabin, perch on the flat sod roof, plop down in front of the clay-plastered wall hung with weasel pelts and wolfskins. They peck at the ground, fly up on a tree, then scold Andrei's intrusion. Another magpie...another and another, fly and dart and flit the same air paths in varied order...all the magpies screeching.

All at once the scene darkens. A cloud blots out whatever

sunlight has been filtering through the green ash leaves. Vityr stiffens, his ears pressed back. He and Andrei step back. Vityr snorts and the toss of his head pulls the twine from Andrei's hand. Brovko whimpers, crawling at Andrei's feet, belly to the ground. Andrei can't be sure, but he thinks he spots a dark form that scurries from back of the cabin into the trees.

Andrei turns away, moving in a fast walk, away from the cabin and out of the grove, back the way they came. They follow the creek bed, past the eroded clay bank all the way to the willow bluffs. From here they climb up the coulee hill. Andrei glances over to the rock. Just a big rock; that's all it is. He'd stop and dig up the goatskin bag if he didn't have to go back to the cellar hole. But really, he's afraid. That will have to be another time.

October

CHAPTER 15

TATO AND DIDO BRING MORE SUPPLIES WITH THEM ON their return from the harvest at Klassen's farm. They bring more flour and sugar, and they bring money. Tato talks to Mama about the things they'll need to purchase for the winter. But more importantly, as far as Marie is concerned, Tato brings a letter from Petrus Shumka. She blushes, and as if all the other things Tato and Dido have brought with them are of no importance whatsoever, she races with the letter to the garden.

"Get away, Andrei. I can see you hiding behind the fence." Marie stands among the hanging heads of sunflowers. She opens her letter with the sharp edge of her thumbnail.

"What does Petrus say?"

"They can't make me marry Wasyl Kuzyk now," Marie says. "Petrus will be here for Christmas."

Andrei breaks off a head from a sunflower. "Petrus is

coming," he yells, running to join Dido sitting on the bench along the south side of the house. The dog runs at Andrei's heels, and chickens peck at potato peels Mama has thrown out the door. Dido holds his willow flute as if contemplating that he might play a note or two.

"Petrus Shumka made a wonderful St. Michael for the play at the harvest festival last year," Dido says. He lifts his flute to his lips and sounds the tune of the Hetman Bayda. He stands up from the bench and proceeds across the yard to the garden. At the willow fence he sings to Marie.

If my Petrus is not in town
A breath of wind may blow me down.
But if his eyes in mine should glance
With arms akimbo watch me dance!
Oh, the trouble he gives, with eyes so bright,
Black moustache and skin so white!

"Go away," Marie says, and she stuffs her letter into a pocket in her dress. She laughs at them and runs through the garden to a gate at the other end. From there she disappears into the trees.

Dido and Andrei walk back to the house. Dido lays his flute on the bench, and reaches into his vest pocket for the pouch containing his clay pipe, his one true Cossack heirloom, with the poppy flowers carved on the bowl. He opens the pouch and rolls the pipe around in his fingers like he always does, as if he's wondering if the Hetman Bayda smoked from a pipe like this. Andrei sits watching the pipe, saying nothing.

"It's good that Petrus is coming," Dido says. "Too bad he's not coming until Christmas. He's so good in plays, and we need to have a good Cossack play to celebrate the harvest. We need to have a harvest festival...we have a church, but no priest. Can we have a harvest festival without a priest to bless the baskets? And we would need a hall to have a play."

Andrei spits out the shell of a sunflower seed. Nobody's house is big enough for a real honest-to-goodness play. A festival would bring people all the way from Wakaw and Alvena. Maybe Gabriel and Chi Pete would come. There is only one building, and that is the church.

"If we had a priest," Dido says, "we'd have a regular church harvest festival. We'd have 'The Blessing of the Fruit.' But Wasyl Kuzyk says a priest can't come from Winnipeg this year. There are too many other parishes to attend."

"So why don't we have a play? And music. Gabriel can bring his Uncle Moise to play the violin. Marie can talk Gabriel into it. Maybe talk him into taking a part. Don't you think so, Dido? Would God be upset if we used the church to put on a play? Don't you think the church is wasted when we have no priest?"

"We have Kuzyk."

"He's no priest," Andrei says. "But we could ask him. He lives right across the road from the church. He takes care of it like he owns it."

"A play for harvest festival...in the church." Dido rolls his flute around in his hands, and then he tugs at his moustache. "What would I do without you, Andrei? What better place to give our thanks?"

"I DON'T KNOW," Mr. Kuzyk says the very next morning, peering upwards at the icons along the face of the choir loft.

"We could have singers up there," Dido says. "Angels! You can be St. Michael, Andrei. Too bad there's not some way to make you fly."

"But the church has been blessed," Mr. Kuzyk says. "When the priest comes from Winnipeg, the cantor sings up there. I sing up there. We can't desecrate Holy objects with a play."

"What is 'desecrate'? Andrei asks.

"Like cursing," Dido says, "or spitting on the altar. We can lug the altar outside behind the church, and the Holy pictures, the banners. But we might be able to use the banner of St. Michael."

"Who will be in this play?" Mr. Kuzyk asks.

"Andrei here, and Marie. Maybe you can be in it, Wasyl."

"And the Smuk boys from Alvena," Andrei says. "They can be the little devils." Robbin, Bobbin, and Dobbin Smuk. They will come for sure. Who would be better in a play than the Smuks?

"Maybe Gabriel," Dido says.

"Sure," Andrei says. "Marie will talk him into it."

"Who will I be?" Mr. Kuzyk asks.

"The big devil," Dido says.

"Devil? How can a cantor be a devil?"

"It doesn't matter," Dido says.

"Of course it matters!" Mr. Kuzyk says. "To be a cantor is to hold a sacred office of the Church. It is the next thing to being the priest."

"For sure," Dido says. "But a play is like a parable in the Bible. The play says one thing, but by that it really means to say something else. So if you do the part of the devil in the play, and if the play is meant to teach the Holy Gospel, then of course you can see how sacred your part in the play really is...you know, like a parable."

For a moment, Mr. Kuzyk scratches his head, but then he nods. "Of course," he says, "even as cantor, my job in the Church is to help spread the Holy Gospel."

CHAPTER 16

By now in their new land, the Baydas think they have reason to feel at least half secure. Their main worry all summer has been whether they'd be able to prepare enough provisions to survive a winter. They still don't know if Mr. Kuzyk exaggerates when he talks about Canadian winters, but at least it seems that firewood is limitless; they shouldn't freeze. They have been luckier than most people, to have a proper house built so they won't have to hunch down in a *buda* like bears their first winter. But they still don't have a plough. Tato decides they will borrow one from Mr. Kuzyk. They'll need the harvest wages to buy enough flour to last the winter. They'll need dried fruit, sugar, and medicines if anyone gets sick. Tato and Dido will want a winter's supply of tobacco. And Tato says it wouldn't be right not to pay off the debt to Sam Zitchka.

It's such a nice time after harvest. Mama says that families will come to the festival even if they won't have a priest there. They will prepare baskets of fruit, vegetables from the gardens, even if there won't be a priest to give the blessings.

The Bayda garden has produced. They have been truly fortunate. They have a milk cow, and the thirteen chicks that hatched in May are already laying eggs. But Mama has been wondering if there will be grain enough to last the winter for them. Surely there will be. The garden plots of barley and wheat produced enough seed to plant at least one or two acres next spring. They'll be pushing it to have two acres ready for planting. There should be enough extra grain to feed fourteen chickens through the winter.

This time of year it's not even that bad to be out in the bush clearing the land. The mosquitoes are gone. So why shouldn't the Bayda's feel like celebrating? On top of everything else, the highbush cranberries are ripe for the picking.

Late in the afternoon, Gabriel Desjarlais rides into the yard. He's brought a haunch of venison. Brovko runs in circles around the horse, barking, and sniffing at the meat.

"Stop it!" Andrei says to the dog.

"Where is everybody?"

"I was in the field picking roots," Andrei says. "Dido's still out there."

"Where's your mother?"

"She's berry picking, and Tato's gone to Kuzyk's to see about borrowing the plough."

"I've brought you some meat," Gabriel says.

"Marie's in the house...she can cook it for supper. I'll take it to her."

"Here," Gabriel says, handing it down to Andrei.

Brovko jumps. "Quit it!" Andrei says, pushing at the dog.

He takes the meat inside, then runs to join Gabriel by the barn.

"Do you think he'll grow as tall as Raven?" Andrei says. Vityr's inside the corral and he approaches the rail, rubbing noses with Gabriel's horse.

Andrei continues with his question. "Don't you think he's growing?"

Gabriel pats Vityr on the neck. "I'm sure," Gabriel says, "he'll be as big as Raven."

Andrei plants his foot on the bottom rail. "Are you busy on Saturday?" he asks.

"Why do you ask?"

"We're having a festival," Andrei says. "Marie's going to be in a play. She wants you to be in it too."

Gabriel starts to laugh. He slaps his knee, asking questions and laughing, each question louder than the first. "You want me to be in a play? A festival? A Ukrainian festival? Marie wants me to act in a play at a Ukrainian festival?"

Marie is standing in the doorway of the house a hundred feet away, a knife and a half-peeled potato in her hands.

"What are you saying?" she shouts. Gabriel turns to face her.

"You want me to be in a play?"

"I never said anything of the kind," Marie says, and she throws the potato in Andrei's direction and stomps back into the house.

"Did I say something wrong?" Gabriel smiles at Andrei, and they walk to the house. Before he gets there, Marie's back in the doorway.

"I baked some buns," she says. "Come inside. And you, Andrei. Maybe I'll give you one, even if you don't deserve it."

They sit around the big trunk in the middle of the east room. They shouldn't be eating in here. The east room is to be used only for special occasions. It will be used for Christmas and Easter, and when visitors come. Gabriel's a vistor, but Mama might not think he's any special kind of visitor, like Mr. Kuzyk and his mother, or like a priest. But Mama might invite Gabriel to this room. She would be thankful for the meat.

"The last thing I want to do," Marie says, "is act in Dido's play."

"Will you, if I go in it?" Gabriel asks.

"You?" Marie stares at him. "You'd actually take a part in a Ukrainian play?"

"Why not?"

"Sure, why not?" Andrei asks. "And Dido has a part for Chi Pete. At our festivals we have music, and dancing too. Dido plays his flute, and he wants the Smuk boys to dance."

"I'll ask Uncle Moise to come. He plays the violin. You haven't seen dancing until you've seen the Red River Jig, and heard Uncle Moise play."

"Dido will tell us what he has in mind. He's been planning all week. After supper we can start practicing." Andrei finishes a second bun. "How long until supper?" he asks Marie. "I have to tell Dido when to come in from the field."

"Tell him in one hour. Go back out and help," Marie says. "I don't want you under my feet when I have work to do." She smiles at Gabriel.

"She'll get you peeling potatoes," Andrei says as he leaves.

CHAPTER 17

THERE'S A SURPRISE. THE BISHOP HAS COME ALL THE WAY from Winnipeg. Mr. Kuzyk found out just three days ago that it was possible for the bishop to come for "The Blessing of the Fruit." The people were to spread the word throughout the district. Get them to come from Alvena. Even as far away as Wakaw.

This is a special occasion. The bishop can't stay long... only five hours. He's on his way to Hafford. It will have to be a Low Mass, and not a High Mass with all the singing. He can baptize seven babies, and stay just long enough for a noon dinner instead of the dinner they had planned to have later in the day. But even if they have the bishop only for five hours, still they can celebrate. Dido can be a Cossack for a day.

The word has got around. Men on horseback appear, wearing fez caps they've dragged out of somewhere, wooden swords, and sashes tied around their waists. They lead the bishop and the banners and all the people in Procession up the trail and three times around the church. Baskets filled with fruit and vegetables, candles, and braided bread covered with white cloths, are strung in two long rows on the grass, as edges for a walkway into the church. Andrei had hoped that Gabriel would ride Raven in the Procession, but he declined. "I'm Métis," he said, "not a Cossack." The men dismount, Dido, Mr. Kuzyk, and the others, and they lead their horses away, tying them to trees. The bishop leads the throng into the church.

AFTER THE MASS, they have half an hour to prepare. The play is set to start at two o'clock. Mr. Kuzyk engineers the removal of the Holy pictures.

"Stack them carefully," he says, "behind the altar where nobody can see them."

Even Tato helps take them down. In ten minutes the church is no longer a church. It is temporarily something else, much like their house was in Zabokruky, where it seemed to lose its home feeling once the pictures were down. With the church walls bared and the bishop gone, the building is now something else, a building suitable for Dido's play.

Andrei climbs the staircase, following three white-sheeted girls dressed as angels. He has St. Michael's banner wrapped around the flagstaff, and he points it straight ahead and above, half crawling in the narrow passage up into the choir loft. He's left Chi Pete and Gabriel outside in the bell-tower shed where they await their entries, Chi Pete as a Scythian warrior, Gabriel, a buffalo hunter.

People are crammed in even here in the choir loft. Andrei worms his way through bodies, passing the wrapped up banner of St. Michael over heads to the girls, fighting his way to the balcony rail. He needs air, and he's sweating hot.

He leans over the rail, grateful for the space. Below him Dido Danylo taps an old lady on the back. She's on her knees, crossing herself and touching her forehead to the floor. He's attemping to keep the aisle open. They need the space for the play. There is no space anywhere else.

The pews are full. The makeshift plank benches behind the pews, and more of these same benches at the front, all the way to the altar, are full. Dido hoped to have the play staged where the altar sits, but it was too wide to get out through the door. People are jammed in shoulder to shoulder, their backs against the wall all the way along both sides of the church.

Dido elbows his way to the front. He raises his arms and begins talking. Andrei can't hear a word. Dido holds both hands high and forward, then pushes down three times as if trying to cram the noise into a box. Andrei concentrates on the lines he's memorized for the play, running them over and over in his mind. And then his stomach tightens as he tries to remember when he's supposed to say them.

"Hey," someone says. Then, "Hey, hey." Here and there a "*Shhh, shhhh.*" Finally the noise dies. Dido thanks the people for coming. He says everyone should thank God for the good harvest. He thanks God and the bishop for letting them use the church. Thanks to Canada for inviting Ukrainians here to farm. Thanks for rain. Thanks for sunshine. He tells the people they should start collecting money to build a hall. He says that after the play the collection plate will be passed around. He welcomes all the Cossack horsemen, thanking them for escorting the bishop in Procession. He scratches his head at the base of his topknot.

Feet begin to shuffle. Someone sneezes. A baby cries.

"Let's have the play," a man's voice calls.

"Yes, yes," Dido says. "And now..." he shouts above a growing din, "the play begins."

He struts down the aisle, flute to his lips, the notes of a melody flitting him out the door.

An old lady whispers. "He plays that thing in a Holy church? It is a sin to play a musical instrument in a Holy church."

Another lady taps her on the shoulder, then points up to the walls. "The Holy pictures are put away," she says.

MARIE'S DRAPED IN A FLOWING RED BLANKET. She wears a crown of purple and yellow flowers. Her thick braid tied with a pink ribbon falls forward down her shoulder. She stands in the aisle, cradling a sheaf of wheat.

The angels sing. From a side room at the front of the church, three boys' heads poke out the doorway, one on top of the other, their faces streaked with charcoal whiskers. Three wooden forks painted black dart in and out from behind the heads.

They race, crawling through people's legs, on their hands and knees under benches. Robbin's rear end pokes into the aisle and he swings his hemp rope tail round and round. Or is it Dobbin, or Bobbin? A rear end appears again, and another, then all three ducking like barn kittens, back under the benches. Around and around they go. In and out.

All at once, from behind the altar, the big devil appears, meeting Marie in the centre of the aisle. Mama has made his costume. She dyed Tato's old underwear a bright red and sewed on a tail. Mr. Kuzyk is twice as thick in the chest and stomach as Tato is. The underwear bulges like a sack of barley ready to split. Mr. Kuzyk's rope tail droops between his legs, dragging on the floor.

"Fair maiden," Mr. Kuzyk says. "Uh, uh..."

"What brings you to my gates?" Dido whispers from outside the back door.

"What brings you to my gates?" Mr. Kuzyk sweeps his arm in a broad gesture toward the altar, then quickly draws his fingers to his mouth, peering up to Andrei on the balcony.

"I am the maiden of bountiful harvest," Marie says, "and I bring food for poor children."

"No, no," Mr. Kuzyk says, "let the children starve. Then no one will believe in God. Share your wheat with me, instead. Feast with the devil and...and...?"

"Feed my greed," prompts Dido.

"Feed my greed."

"I must save the children!" Marie stomps her foot. "Stay away, Devil! Stay away from the children!"

"Yes?" Robbin asks, poking his head out from under a bench.

"Yes?" says Bobbin.

"Yes?" says Dobbin.

"Ahh," Mr. Kuzyk says, "my offspring come to help me." He reaches for the sheaf.

"Wait! Wait! Wait!" Andrei yells from the choir loft. "I am St. Michael, the Archangel. I will send a Cossack to rescue the maiden. A Cossack to give food for all the people."

Dido enters with sabre drawn. He wears his heavy winter sheepskin with a sash at the waist. A tightly-curled fur cap perches on his head and sweat rolls down his cheeks. He's face to face with the red-faced Mr. Kuzyk and the three Smuks, all of them poking their forks. Dido chases them to the foot of the altar. Robbin, Bobbin, and Dobbin form a line in front of Mr. Kuzyk.

"Charge!" say the Smuks, and the chase reverses.

"Oh," says Marie, as Dido pushes her to the side for safety. Andrei waves the banner of St. Michael over everybody's heads. The sabre strikes Robbin's fork, then Bobbin's, then Dobbin's, or the other way around. The three little devils flee to the side room.

Only the big devil remains. He gazes up to Andrei's banner, then thrashes his way to Dido, his fork knocking Dido's sword from his hand.

"I am defeated," Dido says, flat on his back in the aisle, the devil's pitchfork inches from his throat.

"Not defeated," Chi Pete says at the entry. He wears buckskins and moccasins and he wields a wooden sword in one hand, and a knife in the other. A syrup pail is jammed on his head. Andrei couldn't think of anything better for a Scythian helmet. Chi Pete rushes, but stops short at Mr. Kuzyk's roar. He scurries out the door in defeat.

A moment later, Gabriel enters. He stands face to face with the foe, Wasyl posing with his pitchfork aimed at Gabriel's neck. Gabriel shoves forward, armed with a six-foot pole. They feint with their weapons, cutting and thrusting. Marie's at their side, bobbing and weaving with the thrusts. The fighters battle to a standoff, dropping their weapons to the floor, wiping their brows.

"And such is our life," Dido says in the form of an epilogue, rising to his feet to stand between the spent combatants. "Each of us has his own battle within himself. We struggle back and forth with good and evil. Praise God."

Mr. Kuzyk stands up and waves for the Smuk boys to join him. The actors in the aisle bow to each side. Andrei and the other angels bow to the people below. Everyone claps.

"And now," Dido says, "after the collection, we have something really special. Our visitors from Batoche will entertain us outside."

THE YOUNG WOMEN of the community join hands, singing and dancing in a circle, just as they do in the spring during Easter Celebrations. Here they are dancing to the unfamiliar music of the Red River Jig. Gabriel's Uncle Moise, limp arm and all, performs sitting on a stump inside the circle. Uncle Moise bobs his head, topped with his stiff-brimmed hat. He bows and sways to the motions of his violin.

Gabriel glides across the centre of the circle. His feet, clad in laced-up deerskin moccasins, seem unattached, sliding back and forth like Moise's violin bow, making a music in the swishing of leather on grass. His hands are poised on his narrow hips, his back is straight and erect, his head tall, as if only his feet move. His hat, like Uncle Moise's, is black with a wide stiff brim, and the tassels of his red knitted sash twirl at his waist.

Marie dances. Her feet arch, first one, then the other, toes pointing to the ground marking a spot, daring. Her hands poise on her hips, her chin raises, and she twirls twice around, her shirt flaring. Gabriel removes his sash, snaking it through the air as he circles her. They circle each other, wary, their feet thrusting in and out, back and forth, swishing in the grass to the music of the Red River Jig. People are clapping, even Mr. Kuzyk, but his face is red.

Gabriel dances in a wide sweep to the edge of the circle. Chi Pete hands him a branch and he dances back to Marie, his feet always the same, the *swish, swish, swish.* They face each other. He bows, as does she, in the way of a lady, her knee bent and to the side, her back straight and her skirt spread wide. Her hands leave her skirt and come together as Gabriel presents her with the branch of red cranberries.

November

CHAPTER 18

THE POTATOES ARE SAFE IN THE CELLAR, AS ARE THE CARrots, turnips, and beets. In the narrow centre room, bunches of poppy seed pods hang from the ceiling, along with onions, garlic, sacks of dried mushrooms. Six bags of flour are stacked. Pieces of Dido's half-finished loom lean against the wall.

The east room's cold and dark. Tato has just lit a fire in the iron stove, because he and Mama sleep in the east room. Right now, as they do every evening, the whole family congregates in the west room. Supper's done and outdoors the sky darkens. Snow sweeps by the lone window. Flames flicker in the fireplace of the clay stove, adding to the dim light of candles. Marie stands at a table in the centre of the room, dusting flour on dough. On a bench at the north wall, close to the clay stove, Mama leans toward the firelight, mending Dido's fishnet. On the floor beside the table, Tato uses a drawknife to strip bark from willow, crafting Andrei's sled. On his bed against the room's west wall, Andrei braids rope to make a harness for his colt. Dido's stretched out on the clay platform over the stove, for a rare occasion smoking his white clay Cossack pipe.

Andrei's glad it's snowing. Tomorrow morning he'll hitch the colt to the sled. He'll snare rabbits; their trails are easier to find on the snow.

"Don't watch me!" Marie says. She sprinkles more flour, sinks her knuckles into the dough, then rolls it flat into a sheet.

"Who's watching you?" Mama asks.

"All of you!" She flips the sheet of dough, slapping it on the table. She sprinkles poppy seeds, then rolls the dough into a round cake. She will bake it in the clay oven, along with Mama's bread, the unbaked loaves covered with a cloth, set aside on a bench across the room from Mama. This bench too is close to the stove, where the loaves can rise with the warmth of the fire.

LATE INTO THE NIGHT, Andrei lies still. The aroma of baked bread lingers. Dido chokes and sputters, snoring where he sleeps. Mama and Tato have long ago gone to sleep in the other room. Outside, a wolf howls. It stops, then howls again. Andrei's heard wolves before. Mama has always said to watch out for them when he's in the bush. How would you do that? Gabriel says that a wolf would never attack a human, but when Andrei's been out there and he's heard a wolf (or was it coyotes?), the sounds have made him shiver. He's wondered what to do if he comes face to face with a wolf. It's happened with a bear, and that was probably more dangerous.

It howls again. Somehow it's different, but with Dido snoring, Andrei can't be sure. Then he hears something from across the room. It's Marie. She's climbed out of her bed. She's by the fireplace where she wraps the poppy seed roll in a cloth. He hears the shuffle of her sheepskin, the careful creak of the door into the storeroom. She goes outside. Andrei scrapes frost off the window. Moonlight shines on the snow, and Marie steps a path across its whiteness. Andrei thinks he hears the jingle jangle of harness chains, but he's not sure. One thing he knows, it won't be Mr. Kuzyk.

Andrei dreams. He's digging into a pile of potatoes and pulls out the gold cup. Each potato is a cup, each with a vision of fire blazing from its ruby centre. A red horse chases Andrei across a meadow. Vityr shouldn't chase him, or is the colt running with him away from the wolves? It's not wolves, it's a bear, and it swipes at their backs. "Faster!" Andrei says, and they run to hide in the forest. But from deep in the trees, all at once Snow Walker comes at them. Vityr's gone. Andrei stumbles, branches snapping at his face. *Snap! Snap!*

He wakes to a clatter coming from the storeroom. Sticks of wood are falling on top of each other. Marie is bumping and stepping on pieces of Dido's loom. She creaks open the door, tiptoes in the dark across the floor to her bed.

"Marie?"

"Shhh."

"You saw Gabriel?"

"Shhh. Go to sleep. I'll tell you in the morning."

"I had an awful dream, Marie."

"Shhh, don't wake Mama."

But a moment later Mama enters the room. Andrei pretends to be sleeping. Her candle flickers as she proceeds to Marie's bed. Andrei watches, his feather tick tucked to his chin.

"Can you sit up?" Mama says in a whisper. "I heard you come in. Where were you?"

Marie doesn't answer. All that Andrei hears is Dido's snoring.

"Where were you? You think I'm deaf that I can't hear you sneaking in?"

"I went to the toilet."

"Do you have to lie to your mama?" She pulls the cover back on Marie's bed. She sees the red skirt, and a buckskin vest.

"Oi, Marusia. Where did you get that vest? Where were you? You are leaving us, Marusia?"

Marie swings her feet to the floor. She grabs hold of her pillow, clutching it to her lap. "Marie. My name is Marie, and if you have to know, I was at a dance."

"Where at a dance?"

"At Fish Creek."

"There is no hall at Fish Creek."

"At Uncle's Moise's house."

"Since when is he your Uncle Moise?"

"Gabriel's Uncle Moise."

"You don't know what you are doing, Marusia. You're still

young with a full life ahead of you. Please stop and think a little. Think of your future."

"Future? Here? Mama, I don't want to marry Wasyl Kuzyk."

"If you really don't want him, maybe think about Petrus. He is coming here. Petrus is a nice Ukrainian boy. You have your family, Marusia. Don't turn your back on your family."

Andrei thinks that Marie has already made up her mind.

December

CHAPTER 19

EVENINGS ARE GETTING LONGER. IN LESS THAN TWO weeks, it will be the shortest day of the year, and then Christmas. Tato sits on the floor by the fire, a wood mallet in his hand, grinding a cup of poppy seed. Mama sorts kernels of wheat, choosing only the finest. Honey, wheat, and poppy seed will be cooked together for the first dish eaten on Christmas Eve.

"Do you suppose Petrus will arrive in time for Christmas?" Andrei asks.

"Maybe he will," Tato says. "Maybe he won't. But what will you tell him, Marie?" She doesn't answer.

"She'll have to tell Petrus," Mama says. "That's all."

"What can she tell him? That she has her eye on Gabriel?"

"Gabriel? You know better than that. I'm hoping that Marusia will tell him about Wasyl Kuzyk. Without Wasyl Kuzyk, where would we be? He gave us the cow, the hen.

Andrei hopes one day to own a fine colt."

"And he gave me Brovko," Andrei says, trying to be helpful. Would Mama force Marie to marry him? She might run away. Andrei wonders if Petrus would fight Gabriel, and who would win? He's not sure whose side he's on. He likes Gabriel a whole lot, and even if he is of a different people, what difference should that make? Ukrainians have to change their ways here in Canada and not be so stubborn. Petrus would understand. Besides, he'll be so busy with a homestead for himself, he won't have time to even think about Marie. And then if the Holochuk family comes to Canada, there will be more than enough girls to worry about.

"We have to face facts," Tato says. "She doesn't want Kuzyk. The Gabriel fellow is not that bad a catch, even if he's not Ukrainian. Don't you think so, Dido? And didn't a Skomar run off with a Gypsy two hundred years ago? So what if Marie chooses a cowboy instead? But what are we going to tell Petrus?"

"And Wasyl Kuzyk?" Mama asks. "What will we tell Wasyl Kuzyk? And I wish you'd stop calling Marusia that name."

Mama thinks that if the family wants to get ahead, it's better to start with something, not just empty pockets. "All the things Kuzyk did for us," Mama says, "and this is how Marusia shows her gratitude."

"Don't be so hard on her," Tato says. "Canada has all sorts. And if we still lived at our village, would you object if our daughter married a rich Pole?"

"And what would a priest have to say?" Mama asks. "He would say to live by the laws of God. He would say as the

Bible says, that in marriage it is best 'not to go unevenly yoked.'"

Marie clears the supper dishes as if nothing has happened. Andrei knows that she's stubborn, and he's certain she's set on Gabriel.

But now that it's winter the Baydas have other concerns. They had previously only heard stories about Canadian winters. Now they are getting it first-hand. The temperature remains below freezing, and even before December the river was frozen over. The morning after Tato ground the poppy seed, they set out on the river ice to fish.

DIDO FALLS THROUGH THE ICE. He and Tato are setting the net when Dido steps through a muskrat breathing hole and falls into the river. He's soaked to the waist in the ice-cold water. Tato pulls him out, and they run with him, urging him to keep moving, Andrei and Tato each holding a hand, sometimes dragging Dido on the trail home. The horse, Frank, is pulling a sleigh, but they can't let Dido ride. Sitting on the sleigh, he'll freeze before he gets home.

By the time they've covered the three miles to the homestead, Dido's clothes are frozen solid. For the last mile they've had to let him ride. He was encased in his clothes and couldn't move. When they finally get to the house, Tato carries Dido and lays him on a bench in the east room, smack in front of their new metal stove. Mama loads it to the brim with dry split wood. His teeth chatter as Tato helps him remove his clothes. In a few moments he's wrapped in a feather-filled bed covering, shivering and thawing out in front of the roaring stove. From there he's moved to the other room and his sleeping platform over the clay stove.

Every night and day after this, all Dido does is lie on his warm bed. He coughs and coughs. He eats hot bread and garlic cloves, and Mama rubs his chest with goose grease from the Kuzyks. She covers his chest with mustard plasters, and still Dido coughs. One night Mama boils vinegar in the fireplace, sending the fumes to rise up to Dido atop the clay stove. Andrei sees creases on Mama's brow.

"Might Dido die?" Andrei asks.

"I don't know," Mama says.

Never before has Andrei heard Mama say, "I don't know," when someone was sick.

IT'S BEEN WEEKS since they've seen the Kuzyks. Everyone's happy, finally to have company. Even Marie smiles when these neighbours stop in on their way back from Rosthern, just two days before Christmas Eve.

"Christ is born," Mr. Kuzyk says, wiping frost from his moustache.

"Christ is born," his mama repeats, unwrapping a wool scarf from her face and neck.

"He is indeed," Tato says. "Come in. Come in."

He leads them through the door to the east room. Andrei lights the candles on the linen-covered table. The iron stove glows red hot. Tato, Andrei, and Marie sit on rug-covered benches. The Kuzyks sit on the bed, made over to a special couch for day use, perched like statues facing the Baydas. Mama darts back and forth from the kitchen, serving tea, Christmas bread, poppy seed cake, and a small bowl of oranges. They hear Dido coughing from the other room.

"Dido's sick," Mama says.

"Something contagious?" Mr. Kuzyk asks, coughing himself, and covering his mouth.

"He fell through the ice at the river," Tato says. "We were fishing."

"Not a good time for swimming," Mr. Kuzyk says.

"I hope he recovers soon," Mrs. Kuzyk says.

"He's not a young man anymore," Tato says.

"Not like my Wasyl," Mrs. Kuzyk says. She takes a moment to gaze about the room, showing admiration for the Holy pictures hanging on the walls. "You know," and here she looks directly at Marie, "January is a good time for a wedding,"

"You think so?" Tato says. "Marie, go to the cellar. Bring the Christmas wine for the Kuzyks."

"January," Mr. Kuzyk says. "Or the end of December. But for sure not the best time in this country for a cow to have a calf." He laughs, slapping his knee. "How is the cow?"

"I worry about it calving this time of the year," Tato says. "The worst time there could be for a calf to be born."

"Christ was born on Christmas Day," Mr. Kuzyk says.

"In Israel, where it's warm," Tato says.

"She's been a good cow," Mrs. Kuzyk interrupts. "Never any trouble." She keeps her eyes on the doorway Marie walked through to get to the cellar, then pokes her son in the side. "Wasyl has something to ask of you, Mr. Bayda."

Wasyl runs his fingers along his collar, rubbing his neck.

"It's time for me..." he says, then pauses. Mrs. Kuzyk raises her head and smiles to everyone in the room. She beams at her son, placing her hands crosswise on her bosom.

"Aah, aah..." Mr. Kuzyk hesitates. He smiles awkwardly at his mama. She pokes again at his side with her elbow.

"I tell you, Stefan...aah..." and then he blurts out all at once, "your boy has worked hard with my colt. Maybe by next Christmas I'll let Andrei try to ride him. If it wasn't such an expensive horse, I would give it to Andrei, but you know how hard it is to keep your head above water in this farming business."

"I've taught Vityr how to pull a sled," Andrei says. He jumps to his feet and grabs an orange. He takes a slice of poppy seed cake, shoving all of it into his mouth. A third time Mrs. Kuzyk elbows her son. He stands up and walks to the table, takes an orange, and then sits back down on a bench against the wall by the stove. Mama frowns. The oranges cost thirty-five cents for twelve. She'd scolded Tato for squandering money on something she'd never seen before. "It's Christmas," he'd told her. Andrei wonders if there will be any left for Christmas Eve tomorrow. Mr. Kuzyk sucks on the orange. He lifts his head and stares across the room, above the candles to the Holy pictures.

Once more he blurts. "I would like the hand of your..."

At that moment Marie comes up from the cellar and into the room. The wine jug slips from her grasp but she catches it with her other hand. She stands in the middle of the floor, everyone watching to see her reaction to Mr. Kuzyk's request.

She swallows, then blurts out a question.

"Did you see Petrus Shumka at Rosthern?" she asks. "He was to arrive on the train today. He said in his letter..."

Mr. Kuzyk's face turns red and he sweats from the heat radiating off the stove.

"There were so many at the station," Mrs. Kuzyk says.

That's strange, Andrei thinks. Mr. Kuzyk knows very well that Petrus is coming to Canada. Everybody in the district knows.

"You must have seen him," Tato says. "There wouldn't be that many immigrants arriving this time of the year."

Mrs. Kuzyk frowns at her son and then smiles at Mama. "Your poppy seed cake is delicious, Mrs. Bayda."

Mama looks back and forth from Mrs. Kuzyk on the couch to Wasyl by the hot stove. "Were there many, or weren't there many?" she asks.

"Frenchmen," Mr. Kuzyk says. "I think they were all Frenchmen going to Bellevue."

"If they were going to Bellevue," Tato says, "they would get off the train at Duck Lake."

"Was there one young man?" Marie asks. "Dressed like a Ukrainian?"

"More than one young man," Mrs. Kuzyk says. "How would we know how they dress?"

"Can't you see?" Marie asks. "Petrus said he would be here today. If he didn't come today, he might come tomorrow."

Mr. Kuzyk sucks once more on his orange. The next moment he starts to cough. His face turns redder and his whole body shakes. Tato hurries to him with a glass of wine. He drinks, wipes his brow, and hands back the empty glass.

"I talked to someone," Mr. Kuzyk says. "I think he might have said he came from district Horodenka."

"Horodenka?" Mama asks.

"Said he was going to find somebody's place. I don't know if he might have said *Baydas.* Mama was in a hurry. I didn't listen."

"Did he ask where to go?" Tato stands over Mr. Kuzyk, his hand and empty glass bobbing slowly up and down.

"He came with us as far as the river. Maybe he said *Bayda.* Aren't there Baydas north of Fish Creek? I told him to go north."

"You did what?" Tato asks. "He could get lost up there!"

"North?" Marie says. "North? Why would you tell him that? This isn't Horodenka. Here there are miles and miles of nothing but bush. Petrus could be lost. He could freeze before he'd find anybody."

"That's on the way to Batoche," Andrei says. "Maybe Petrus will run into Chi Pete."

"Wasyl," Tato says, pointing a finger at Mr. Kuzyk, standing over him where he sits red-faced. Mr. Kuzyk coughs, glances over to his mother, peeks at Marie, then peers down at the floor.

"To go north is not miles and miles of nothing," Mr. Kuzyk says. "There are French people along the river all the way past Batoche. Gabriel's people are there. If it is this Petrus, he might even find some work to do there. Something temporary. What's wrong with that? Who here among us can afford to feed someone all winter?"

Mr. Kuzyk's face keeps getting redder and redder. He glances from his mother to the door.

"I have chores to do at home," he says.

"Yes," Tato says. "You better go."

CHAPTER 20

More snow has fallen through the night. The morning sky looms high and clear, tinged a metallic blue-grey. The air is absolutely still. A woodpecker rattles on a tree somewhere near. A mouse runs a ridge through the snow, on top yet not on top, a rolling line on its way to the trees and disappearing. Andrei takes a frozen fish from the crate stored in the *buda* and calls for the dog.

"Here, Brovko! Here, Brovko, Brovko!" He calls several times. Finally the dog appears straggling from the barn, hair over his eyes, head low to the ground, ears laid back, tail dragging, wagging feebly through the snow, as if the dog knows something is going to happen. A change in the weather. Something dangerous. It takes the fish in its mouth and scurries back to the barn.

Andrei will take Vityr with him to go look for Petrus. The venture will at least help take his mind off Dido's sickness. The spirit of Christmas is dim. Before Dido got sick, everyone so looked forward to Christmas in Canada. But now it's constant worry. Last night Mama scolded, "We've had things too good." She even scolded Tato. "When we left our comfortable home, you thought we were going to a land of milk and honey. Here we don't even have a graveyard."

Christmas has made everybody a little bit lonely for the old homeland. And now Dido might die. Andrei has always gone with questions to his dido. The two of them share the secret of the cup, and Andrei wants his dido with him to learn more of its magic. What could Andrei possibly do all by himself?

Last night Dido's cough gurgled, and he spit blood. Mama killed one of the young chickens and made a broth for him. She tried the ancient remedies; prayed as she melted wax into a cup of water held over his head. Nothing worked. She said that misfortune was fully upon them. She had looked forward to seeing Petrus, to hear first-hand news from the home village, and now where was he? Probably lost somewhere in the bush. Mama heated a bag of damp barley in the oven. She gave it to Andrei to lay over Dido's throat. She thought the added heat might break his fever.

Dido's head turned to Andrei's ear. "The cup, Andrei."

THIS MORNING Andrei's draped in Dido's sheepskin coat.

"Where are you going?" Mama asks from the doorstep as he follows Brovko's tracks to the barn.

"Vityr and I are going with the sled. There's lots of snow for a good ride. I'm going to check the rabbit snares." He doesn't mention the cup.

"And look for Petrus?" Mama asks. "Do you think you should go? Don't you think Petrus will find somebody who knows where we live?"

She sweeps snow from the step, then peers up at the sky, and at the white snow all around. She asks again, "Do you think somebody will tell him where we live?" The creases on her brow are more pronounced than ever.

AN ODD SNOWFLAKE FALLS. The blue-grey dome of sky seems a shade darker. Bundled in the heavy sheepskin, and with the black and white and grey leafless trees hovering on each side of the narrow trail, Andrei feels closed in.

Vityr steps along sleigh tracks filled with last night's snow. They stop a minute by a highbush cranberry. The shrub still has fruit, the berries glistening a bright red. Andrei eats a few. They're full of juice. Some drop off into the snow, and he steps on them, the snow staining as if it bleeds.

A feather of new snow swirls in a circle on the trail. More snowflakes fall from the sky, more hurried, not floating as before. Snow feathers along the path in swirls of twos and threes, each one chasing the next, the wind seeming to blow from above Andrei's head. Soon the forest thins to bluffs and rolling hills. Here the wind gusts from all directions, but mostly from the north.

Vityr comes to a stop all on his own. Andrei hears the storm, at first only faint, now and then a whisper in the swirls. But now on the open prairie, Andrei and the colt are fully exposed to the wind and snow. Sheets of it sweep down to strike and then rise retreating, only to sweep back, repeating over and over until the motion is constant, a steady moving blast of snow, moans and screams of snow sucking at Andrei's breath. Vityr hangs his head, turning away from the storm.

Andrei unhooks the harness from the sled, discarding it and leading the colt. He has no idea where they are, all sense of direction lost. Even up and down look the same. The snow clings to Andrei's face.

Both he and the colt are in snow up to their knees. Andrei stumbles, falling on Vityr's neck. The colt's four feet pump then hesitate, stilt-like in the snow. Andrei grabs a line of the harness draped on Vityr's back, then pats the colt on the rump. He has to forget about the cup, forget about looking for Petrus, and instead let Vityr lead them home. He slaps Vityr's rump, but the colt doesn't budge. Now what are they to do?

Andrei takes the lead rope again, and tugs at Vityr's halter. He ties the rope around his own waist and the two of them plunge on through the storm.

They're on a hillside, half walking, half stumbling, moving downward, the wind at their backs. Though he can't see anything but the blizzard, Andrei figures they're moving south, and not toward home. But he won't go back uphill and into the wind. All they can hope for is to find trees. Find shelter somewhere below.

A sound pierces, cutting like a knife through ice, a high-pitched and sweeping wail, as if calling *"Heeere! Heeere!* Andrei almost runs, stumbling, pushed forward and down by the wind, the tug of Vityr's halter pulling at his back. He loses his footing all at once. The ground has given way and he's up to his neck in snow. He falls forward, his hands reaching ahead, hitting a wall. Rock. He's stumbled upon the Indian rock. Thank goodness, he thinks. At last he knows where he is...he's come to the cup after all.

Andrei unties the rope from his waist, then crawls through the snow to the back of the rock. He can feel the heat of Vityr's breath at his neck. On his knees, Andrei brushes away snow, revealing the small pile of stones stacked at the rock's base. He pries a stone loose and pounds it against the others, breaking the frozen heap apart. The snow swoops down the hillside to the rock then curls each way, forming banks at the sides. Andrei pries out shale, one piece at a time, laying the pieces flat on the ground. He reaches into the hole and pulls out the goatskin bag. He removes the lacquered box, setting it down on the shale. Andrei forgets the cold. The clinging snow melts on his forehead, water running down his cheeks, and then the premonition...the sudden twitch of his temple. The storm calms.

He flicks open the clasp and lifts the lid. He unwraps the cup, spreads the black cloth on a blanket of snow. A black feather rests on the ruby jewel at the centre. The feather can't belong. Andrei pulls it out and drops it in the snow. Slowly a golden halo of light rises from the cup, the spray of red glowing at its centre, rising from the ruby jewel. The six golden horse heads twirl in a circle.

Andrei shuts his eyes. Out here he can't allow himself to be drawn to magic. Out here he's in danger of freezing to death. He must keep hold of his senses.

But he feels a persistent twitching on his temple, and warmth rising from the ground. Opening his eyes he picks up the cup and holds it to his chest, then extends it out before his eyes. Gold stars and red moons twirl inside the cup. A miniature Scythian warrior, the very picture of Andrei, clings to the ruby, his arms extended, holding the lines of the six horses that form the cup.

Andrei places it on top of the rock. The cup separates. The six horse heads line up in a row, and the Scythian rides a ruby chariot, driving the horses west along the ridge.

Andrei follows it to the west end of the rock, where he picks it up, back in its original shape. He fills the cup with snow, and the red light rises, melting snow to water. Andrei pours water into the mouth-shaped crevice of the buffalo stone. Three times he pours water where it turns to ice on the granite face. He then points the cup directly at the rock. A flame shoots from the crevice back and forth to the cup.

From somewhere out of the noise and swirling snow of the storm, Andrei hears rattles and the growling of a bear. The colt rears up in the swirling snow, neighing again and again. He leaps through drifts, galloping up the hill into the wind. Andrei hears Vityr's scream, and the moan of the wind, fade and disappear over the hillside. He clutches the cup tight to his chest.

CHAPTER 21

EVEN IF HE HAS THE CUP, ANDREI KNOWS HE CAN'T STAY exposed out here at the rock. He's got to find shelter somewhere below, a place out of the wind where there's wood for a fire. He sits with his back to the rock, fingers wrapping the cup in the black cloth, placing it into the box. He snaps the lid shut and stuffs the treasure into the goatskin bag.

Andrei wonders about the cup's power. Can it be of help? Dido wants it, but it's Andrei who needs the help now. Was it just luck, or was it the cup's power that brought him to the rock? At least now he knows where he is. Vityr's gone, but a horse should survive in a storm. He'll probably find his way back to the barn. Andrei can't see past his nose, but at least he knows there's bush for shelter somewhere at the bottom of the hill.

He shakes snow from his woolen hat and puts it back on, tugging it low over his forehead and ears. Dido's sheepskin keeps him warm, but it hangs heavy on him, more and more coated with the clinging snow. The further he walks, the deeper the snow gets. Andrei can't see a foot ahead. He drags the goatskin bag trailing over snow, his free hand ahead to catch himself when he stumbles. The snow is halfway up his thighs.

Andrei's no longer sure that he's moving downhill. The wind howls louder than ever, the choking snow swirling around him blasts thicker than ever. He should be coming to the bluffs, but it seems that, if anything, he's even more exposed. The only good thing is that the snow seems not so deep. But why? It should be deeper at the bottom of the hill. The snow should bank up against the bluffs.

Andrei's boots slide on ice and he nearly falls. Suddenly he understands. Ice, he's on the ice. He's on the river! And he doesn't know how long he's been on it.

He missed the willows. He's got to get back there. He's got to get off the river. It's like Andrei's fallen off the earth, his only mooring the goatskin bag gripped in his mitt.

He's got to rest. Hunching down, he takes off his mitts and wipes ice and snow from his face. He's got to get off the river, but where? He has no sense of how long he's been wandering. The wind is at his back. He calculates that the wind is blowing from the north if it hasn't changed. That would mean he's facing south, and the shore should be to his left.

It's easier walking now. The snow's not more than a foot deep, and in places he's sliding on bare ice. On he goes, further and further, still on the river, struggling to stay on his feet, buffeted by the force of the wind. Why hasn't he reached the shore? Maybe the river bends. Maybe it's running east and west, and not north and south. Or maybe the wind has changed direction. He remembers the Gypsy fortune teller and her crystal ball. She had told him that the gold turned to nothing but white...

Andrei drops to his knees. He'll rest again. He wishes he had something to eat. Reaching into the pocket inside Dido's coat, he grabs onto a cloth bag. It's Dido's Cossack pipe. He wishes it could be a crust of bread instead. Andrei eats snow, and cradles the goatskin bag. He's got to keep walking. If he sits here, he will freeze to death. On and on he trudges, blind to any direction, aware only of the need to keep the icy wind to his back.

Andrei hasn't thought of the danger of falling through the ice. He hasn't thought of muskrat breathing holes, and it wouldn't have mattered because he wouldn't have seen the danger anyway, until it was too late. He doesn't see it when it does happen, only hears the cracking of ice as it gives way.

He's splashing in water up to his neck, his feet barely able to reach bottom. Arms thrash in ice and slush and chilling water. The goatskin bag floats in front of him. Andrei reaches into it for the box. He takes out the cup, holding it up. The dazzle of its beauty is as bright as ever, this time Andrei seeing it as it really is, the cup a circle of reined-in horses, spinning as if in a whirlwind, the ruby in its eye.

A sense of quiet settles over Andrei with the twitching of his temple. It seems that the blood-red ray ascending from the cup warms him. The vision grows as the Scythian warrior rises from his horse into the sky.

"No!" he thinks. "No! No!" and in a last flash of consciousness, he flings the cup into the storm.

Andrei's rejected the Scythian cup, and it's only now that

he begins to hear the rattle. Above the splash of ice-cold water, the blasts of wind-swept snow, Andrei hears for a moment the clattering of Snow Walker's dewclaw rattle. He swallows water, coughs, and wonders if this is what it is to die. He's no longer cold, and he falls into a calming sleep.

And then he slowly wakes, the time an hour or an instant...he doesn't know which. Andrei feels the pinch of sharp claws clinging at his sheepskin, and he's dragged from the water up onto the ice. The next thing he does know, he's standing alone on the surface of the ice.

All at once he notices that the wind blows warm, a thawing wind, the snow sticking more than ever to his clothes. Again for a brief moment he hears a rattle and sees a black form ahead, cutting through the curtain of snow. He hears growling, as if a bear's shadow calls him to follow. But what would a bear be doing out in the winter? And why would it be helping Andrei? But then he remembers seeing the bear that day at the rock. Whatever is happening, Andrei doesn't have much choice but to follow. The wind is at his back, and every few moments the dark figure shows through the choking blanket of snow.

He walks to keep his circulation, keep from freezing in his wet clothes, boots sliding on ice, tramping through drifts, gripping on crusts...gripping on crusts...deeper snow...

There's no more ice! He's in a snowbank up to his thighs. Shoreline, and high banks against willows. Andrei grabs hold of branches, using them to pull himself along. Waist deep in snow, he plunges on through willows. After a while he's more and more certain where he is. Once through the willows, he makes out a high cliff to his right. He comes to

the grove of twisted trees, and the cabin.

He doesn't know if he opens the door, or if it is opened for him. All he knows is that a hot fire burns in a tin stove. He stumbles to it, a boy inside a mass of ice-stiff sheepskin. Snow Walker takes him by the arm and sits him down in a chair by the stove, helps him remove his frozen clothing.

Andrei shivers, wrapped in a blanket, absorbing heat from the stove. Boiling water bubbles in a blackened tea can on the tin stove. Snow Walker pours tea into a tin cup and he spoons in sugar. He passes the cup to Andrei. The tea is hot and sweet, warming his stomach, giving him energy, lessening his shivers. Only after Andrei finishes the tea does Snow Walker feed him. He dishes stew into a blue enamel bowl and hands it to Andrei, who spoons the meat stew into his mouth. For a moment Snow Walker watches him eat, then passes him a slice of bannock, a saucer of corn syrup, and another cup of the hot tea.

Neither says anything. The time before, when Andrei met with Snow Walker, it was Chi Pete who translated. The silence doesn't seem to matter. The only sound is the snap of the fire and the drip of water from Dido's sheepskin hanging from a beam on the ceiling. After an hour, Andrei's finally warm. Snow Walker spreads wolfskins on a willow cot. He says something in Cree, and points for Andrei to lie down.

The drips of water from the sheepskin have formed a small puddle by the stove. The ice has melted from the coat. The heat from the stove, and the wet wool emit a scorched smell of comfort. Andrei stands up and reaches into the inside pocket of the coat. He takes out the little bag and hands it to Snow Walker.

The pipe glistens in the firelight. Snow Walker lays it in the palm of his hand. He strokes the poppy flower engravings on each side of the cup. Turns it round and round in his fingers like Dido does. Lifts the pipe to his nose. Only then does he put the pipe back in the bag, to hand back to Andrei.

"No, no," Andrei says, holding his hands up, indicating for Snow Walker to keep it, that the Cossack pipe is a gift. Andrei's sure that Dido wouldn't mind. It just seems right that Snow Walker should have it; Andrei doesn't have anything else to give.

ANDREI SLEEPS through the rest of the day, all night, and most of the next morning. When he wakes, it's noon. A small table sits by the cot. His clothing is dry and draped over a chair. On the table are the Cossack pipe, a package of tobacco, and a weasel skin bundle. Snow Walker stands at the other end of the table. He takes tobacco in one hand, and the pipe in the other, nods at Andrei, then draws his hands together. Andrei squints. Snow Walker gestures again that he wants to fill the pipe and smoke it. Andrei nods as if speaking for his dido.

Snow Walker takes a pan of embers from the stove and places a length of braided grass on the coals. Smoke issues and he lets it rise through his hands holding the clay pipe. He lets it pass over the weasel skin bundle, and then he lights the pipe, drawing the tobacco smoke four times. He speaks in Cree, but not to Andrei. He speaks skyward, the Cossack pipe raised toward the ceiling.

It's only after this ceremony that he opens the weasel skin. Inside it are a black feather, a square of red flannel, and a bear claw. Snow Walker places the white clay pipe in the bundle, tying it closed. There's nothing more. Andrei thinks it must be time for him to leave. The storm's over and he's anxious to get home. The family must be worried sick. And the colt! He'd give anything if only Vityr made it home! Sunlight streams through the window. He dresses. Snow Walker feeds him tea and bannock.

When Andrei finishes eating, he puts on the sheepskin and his hat, holds his mitts in one hand, and in the centre of cabin, stands face to face with Snow Walker. He extends his right hand, touching Snow Walker's elbow. He wants to embrace him, but Andrei doesn't know if that's what he should do to show his thanks to a Cree medicine man. With both hands, Snow Walker grasps Andrei's arm, nods, and a grin breaks across the creases of his leathery face. He hands Andrei another piece of bannock to put in his pocket, and opens the door. Andrei's now ready to go home.

The forest outside is nothing that he remembers. Last night he paid attention only to the black form leading him. He'd seen this place before, but it was in the summer. This morning everything's banked with snow, but at least the wind has died.

A squirrel chatters high up on a branch. The snow's deep, but Andrei thinks he knows the way. Some of the terrain he recognizes from the summer. The high cliff on his left, the willow shrubs ahead. Soon he's through the willows and knows for sure that he's at the bottom of the coulee. It's then he hears the jingle-jangle of bells. A horse and sleigh appear at the top of the hill.

"Hey!" Andrei yells, waving his arms. It's Gabriel and Chi Pete! And someone else is with them. Someone wearing an Old Country hat. It has to be Petrus. "Hey! Hey! Down here. I'm down here!"

They leave the sleigh at the top, running to meet Andrei more than halfway down the hill. "Andrei!" Gabriel cries, grabbing the boy's shoulders with a shake and then a hug.

"Petrus!" Andrei says. "What's Petrus doing here?" Andrei and Petrus hug each other, over and over.

"Thank God you are safe!" Petrus says. "Chi Pete thought you might be around here somewhere."

"We were taking Petrus to your place," Gabriel says.

"He came to Batoche yesterday," Chi Pete says. "Right to the store. I asked him who he was looking for, and he said 'Stefan Bayda.' So we set out, early this morning."

"We met your father on the trail," Gabriel says. "He'd been searching for you half the night. 'Thank God you found Petrus,' he said. 'You know the country better than I do,' he said. 'Find Andrei!' Your father said he had been in the barn with the cow...three o'clock in the morning when your horse appeared out of the storm. Your father left the cow struggling to have its calf, and he went looking for you. When he met us, he kept repeating, 'Please find Andrei.' And then he said that if the cow died, everybody might perish before the Canadian winter finished its work."

"So Vityr's in the barn," Andrei says.

"So your father told us," Chi Pete says.

Petrus steps between them. His smile is as bright as the sun. "I'm glad I didn't come all the way to Canada just to find you frozen to death." He hugs Andrei again, cheek to cheek, one side then the other. Petrus's hat falls in the snow.

"My God! What a country this is!" Petrus says, tromping in snow above his knees.

"Your hat," Andrei says, holding back from laughing.

"What's wrong?" Petrus asks. "It's the same hat I always wear."

"Sure," Andrei says. "Nothing wrong with your hat. Nothing wrong with that hat, is there, Chi Pete?"

"Not that I can see," Chi Pete says. "Is something supposed to be wrong with it?"

"Of course not," Andrei says. It's less than a year they've been in Canada, and already, Petrus's floppy hat with its colourful band seems so strange. Andrei picks it up, brushing off snow.

"I bet that Mother will have the Christmas Eve supper waiting for us," Andrei says.

Gabriel points to the big rock. "You see that, Petrus? The Cree people, the people who were always here, see it as a shrine. A place of retreat. A place where the Great Spirit lives."

"Just a minute," Andrei says. "I have to do something. It won't take long." He slides down the drift of snow into the depression at the base of the rock. He takes the brass button from his pocket, walks to the west end of the rock, and inserts the button into the crevice where he found it in the spring, a time that seems ages ago.

CHAPTER 22

MR. KUZYK'S TEAM STANDS HITCHED TO A TREE IN Bayda's yard. Andrei runs to the barn to see if Vityr's there for sure, then hurries to the house. Mama's at the doorway, her hands clutching her apron to her bosom. "Come in, come in," she says. Andrei hugs his mother, then runs by her into the storeroom, to the entry of the east room, the special room for guests and holidays. He can't believe his eyes. Seated with the others in the room are Tekla Holochuk, and Petrus's sister Martha.

"*Oi, oi,*" Mama says, her eyes filling with tears. She rocks from one leg to the other, as if uncertain what to do do first... express her joy for the return of Andrei, or announce to his rescuers the arrival of the unexpected company.

Mr. Kuzyk rises from a bench at the side of the Christmas table. It's the Bayda trunk, resting in place against the east wall, under the Holy pictures. The trunk is a shrine now at Christmas, the centre-piece of the room, covered with linen, candles, and food. Mr. Kuzyk's mother and Martha Shumka remain seated. "Christ is born," he says.

"Glorify Him," Petrus says, and he waves to everybody in the room.

Mr. Kuzyk approaches Petrus, and a silence fills the room. Mrs. Kuzyk's hands rise to her face. Andrei can see that her son's head appears to sink even further into his neck, as if attempting to bury itself between his shoulders.

"You made it here," Mr. Kuzyk says, then glances at Marie, and then at Petrus's sister, Martha, and from her eyes seems to gain the courage to speak more. "I'm sorry I sent you north. I didn't know that a storm would come. I am so ashamed. So much so, that I wouldn't even have had the strength to come here today, had it not been to deliver Tekla and your sister. I am Wasyl Kuzyk," he says, and he holds out his hand.

"And I am Petrus Shumka." They shake hands.

Marie breaks the stillness. She runs up to the entry and hugs Andrei.

"We were so worried...we thought you would die in that storm." Then she turns to Petrus.

"Christ is born," she says, voicing the Christmas greeting. She lowers her eyes and her complexion gets rosy.

"Glorify Him," Petrus says again. He steps toward her, then all at once, Tekla shoots up from where she's sitting, on Tato and Mama's bed made into a bench on the north wall, close to the iron stove. Quick as a flash she's at Marie's side...a half-step ahead, in fact. At this moment another voice is heard.

"Christ is born." Dido appears from the other room. On his head he wears a wool knit cap that hides his braid. He wears his white linen shirt, embroidered at the neck and down the sleeves, and his wide Cossack trousers. Dido wobbles. Both hands shake, gripped to a walking stick. Mama meets him and settles him down to sit near the stove. He coughs, then wipes spittle from his lips with his sleeve. Andrei comes to him, arms wide, Dido raising his, both arms shaking, and they embrace.

"The golden cup?" Dido asks.

Mama stands between them, holding a bowl of chicken broth for Dido. "Our boy was lost in the blizzard," she says, "and you're asking him for things from the Devil?"

Dido doesn't answer her. Either he can't hear, or his illness has weakened him both in body and mind; as if his thoughts have strayed as far back as to the Holy man Skomar, and the Cossack hillside of his homeland.

"I got it," Andrei answers him, "but it's gone."

"Gone?" With one hand Dido takes the soup from Mama, and dismisses her with the other. Dido and Andrei sit together, side by side.

"I fell through the ice with it," Andrei says. "On the river. I threw it. The cup is at the bottom of the river."

"You fell through the ice? Like me? How did you get out? How did you stay alive in that storm?"

"The Indian medicine man, Dido. He turned himself into a black bear, and he dragged me from the water."

"You mean that Snow Walker you talk about?"

"Yes, Dido."

For several moments Dido glances about the room. Everyone is silent.

Finally Mama says something. "Come inside and shut the door," she says to Gabriel. "Come inside. You don't have to take off your moccasins. Wipe the snow off with a rag. Come in. Everybody sit down. Everybody must be hungry. It won't be long and we will eat."

"Snow Walker saved me," Andrei says.

"How come you didn't freeze solid? Look how sick I got."

"You are old, Dido. And it wasn't really that cold. Just the snow and the wind. And then the wind came warm. Something kept me moving. Snow Walker took me to the warmth of his cabin. I gave him your pipe, Dido."

Andrei's grandfather feels in his pockets. His eyebrows pinch and his moustache rotates with the working of his lips. "Turned himself into a bear?" he asks, more to himself than to Andrei. He reaches, pointing for Andrei to pass him his flute. He takes it and rolls it round and round in his fingers as he would the clay pipe.

"The Snow Walker saved your life as a Cossack would have done," Dido says. "He saved your young life that you may grow into a man in this new land. Here there are heroes other than Cossacks. There can be heroes of all colours and races in a land of all colours and races. Here it is not like in our old Ukraine, where our Cossacks had enemies in every direction...Turks, Poles, Russians. And what did it get us? Great horsemen. Blood shed with sabres. Has that kept our Ukraine alive? No, Andrei, it is our poets who keep Ukraine alive." He plays a few notes of the song of the Hetman Bayda.

"Here, Andrei, in Canada, it's only your old dido who's still a Cossack. Here the people will be mixed together. Already you have a friend, Chi Pete. Let the cup sink into the river sand."

Mr. Kuzyk coughs louder than normal, as if to call

everyone's attention to him, and away from Dido.

"Andrei," he says. "So you went out in the storm to look for your friend?"

"It wasn't storming when I left the yard," Andrei says.

"You took Vityr with you?"

"Yes," Andrei says.

"You could have been killed," Mr. Kuzyk says.

"Vityr made it back to the barn," Andrei says.

"I wasn't worried about Vityr. A horse can survive in a blizzard." Everyone nods, and for the third time the room is silent. "It was my fault that your life was in danger."

"Please don't worry any more, Mr. Kuzyk. I'm fine. Everything is fine."

"But you have done even more than a fine thing, Andrei. And because of it, I want you to have the colt. I want you to have Vityr. He is yours."

Andrei hears it and he's numb. What else can happen? There's nothing he can say, only that he's happy, happy, happy. Nothing he can do, nothing but what Petrus did – the honourable thing – and hold out his hand, shake the hand of Wasyl Kuzyk. Shake the hand of a good and generous man who only made a mistake because he wanted nothing more in life than a good wife to be his companion.

"Christ is born," Andrei says, and he shakes Wasyl Kuzyk's hand.

Andrei walks over to sit down on a bench by the trunk. I am home, he thinks, and I have Vityr. Here I am safe in this house at Christmas, here safe in this country, and after my danger in the river, safe from frightful visions.

"Come, the rest of you, and sit down!" Mama says. "Come, Petrus. And you Gabriel. You don't have to stand. Look, Petrus, your sister has come. See her helping already with the supper." Martha Shumka slices the decorated Christmas bread and arranges it on a tray. Mr. Kuzyk watches her. When she glances at him, her face turns a deep red.

"I was so worried about Andrei," Mama says. "What was I to do about the supper with him lost out there somewhere in the snow? Thank God you found him, Gabriel." She crosses herself.

"All in all, it might even have been a little of a good thing," Mr. Kuzyk says, "that Petrus walked north to Batoche. See how he brought Gabriel to find Andrei. Glory be to God!"

The room is silent again for a moment, but Martha Shumka lowers her eyes and smiles at Mr. Kuzyk.

"And look what I found today," he says. "Mama made me take her all the way to Rosthern this morning just to see if any Christmas mail had arrived. And there standing on the station platform were these girls, Martha and Tekla, looking lost on the platform. I asked them their names, and who they were looking for." He beams at Martha. "And they said they had to find the Baydas. Mysterious are the Lord's ways that I would be there to bring them here."

"Look Andrei. At Tekla's headscarf," Marie says. "Natasha did the embroidery. She made it for a going-away present."

"Oh," Petrus says. "Natasha! You should see how she's grown over the summer. She's become a fine young woman!"

Everybody looks at Andrei.

"Ah," Andrei says to Chi Pete. "Just a girl I used to know

in the Old Country."

Petrus laughs, then tells how he got separated from Martha and Tekla on the journey across Canada.

"I left the girls," Petrus says, "at, what was it...Winnipeg? A cousin of Tekla's was there to meet us. 'You stay,' I said. 'I'll go and you come later.' I didn't expect them this soon."

All this time, Andrei notices that Marie has been watching Petrus. He sees too that Mama notices. She talks to Mrs. Kuzyk.

"Marusia," Mama says to the old woman, "and Petrus..." Mama smiles. "They used to be childhood sweethearts. Of course, a lot has happened since we moved to Canada. She has met other boys." At this point Mama pats Mr. Kuzyk's shoulder. Mrs. Kuzyk smiles in return and nods her head.

"Petrus," Marie says, glaring at Mama, then smiling at him, "can I talk to you?" From where she sits, Tekla Holochuk glowers at Petrus. He flinches, then shrugs, rises from the bench and follows Marie into the storage room. By its entry, Andrei listens and watches. Petrus and Marie stand beside the loom, facing each other, but avoiding each other's eyes.

"I have something to tell you," Marie says. She fiddles with the patterned flower embroidered on the sleeve of her blouse.

"No," Petrus says. "Don't tell me anything! A lot has happened since you left the village." Marie peeks upward just for a moment, her eyes locking on the bobbing of Petrus's Adam's apple.

"You see," Petrus says, "Tekla and I..."

"Tekla?" questions Marie. "What do you mean, Tekla? You have an interest...?"

"I'm sorry," Petrus says.

"No! No, that's quite all right. I don't mind. You see, I don't mind."

"You don't?" Petrus stares at her. "You don't? You don't?" and then his face lights up in a smile. "You can be Tekla's bridesmaid..."

"You're getting married? Oh, Petrus..."

"You just said you don't mind..."

"Of course! Of course!" Marie says, herself smiling. "Of course I can be bridesmaid."

"And you said in your letter that Mr. Kuzyk wants a man to cut bush for him this winter. I came here to do that. In the spring Tekla and I plan to marry, and we can start on a homestead. I already have the land papers."

"Oh, that's wonderful, Petrus. I'm so happy for you. Really, I am."

They step back into the east room. Marie walks over and sits by Gabriel, taking his hand. Petrus joins Tekla. Mama turns this way and that in the centre of the room, finally approaching Mr. Kuzyk and his mother. Mama's hands are extended open, low at her sides. Her head bows as if apologizing.

"It's all right," Mr. Kuzyk says. "All right. Martha is coming to our home. We need help with the housework. You are coming, aren't you, Martha?"

Petrus's sister, Martha Shumka, lowers her eyes again, for how many times Andrei doesn't know, and she blushes and nods.

"You see?" Mr. Kuzyk says. "And then in the spring..."

Mrs. Kuzyk pats herself on the lap with her plump hands. "A long time ago I was married in the spring," she says. "A lovely time for a wedding...all the green just coming. Might there be another? Hey, Wasyl." Martha Shumka blushes all the more.

"Anybody want to play cards?" Mr. Kuzyk says.

"Not today," his mother says. "Nobody wants to play cards on Christmas Eve."

Dido takes up his flute and plays a few notes. He sets it down again and hums to the tune of the Hetman Bayda.

"All is settled then?" Tato asks. "Go, Andrei. Watch in the sky for the first star. Then we can partake of our meal for Christmas Eve."

Andrei and Chi Pete will watch for the Christmas star. It's dusk, and very soon the star will appear. Andrei takes two slices from the tray of Mama's Christmas bread.

The ground cover of snow has taken on the shadows of early evening. The boys walk to the barn. Raven stands, still hitched to the sleigh, eating from a pile of hay that Gabriel has placed on the snow. Andrei gives Chi Pete a slice of the bread for Raven and takes the other piece into the barn. Brovko wags his tail. He's curled up beside the oxen, in a pile of hay at the far end of the barn.

Andrei's face to face with Vityr and nuzzles him cheek to cheek, arms around the colt's neck. Andrei repeats the embrace on the other side of Vityr's long nose, like two old men would hug, but for Andrei this hug's not ritual, but one of joy that they are home safe together. Andrei feeds the colt the Christmas bread, then leads Vitryr out of the barn.

The two horses nibble at the hay. The boys stand beside them, watching the sky.

ACKNOWLEDGEMENTS

MY RESEARCH FOR THIS BOOK COINCIDED from start to finish with its writing. Two days before the disk went to those at Coteau Books who prepare the galley proofs, I was phoning for the detail on ferry boats to Allister Bishop in Lucky Lake, whose father in the early days ran the Riverhurst Ferry. My extended year as Writer-in-Residence in the Quill Plains had me sounding off chapters to students in sixteen schools, had me composing scenes for the book during the writing workshops. Taras Bayda (with the title HETMAN on his license plates) toured me through the setting of the story. John Zrymiak, my long ago school teacher when I was Andrei's age, helped me now with Ukrainianisms. The late Kokum Stella from the Fishing Lake First Nation, told me (among other things) how her people referred to the third stomach of a moose as the bible. Maria Campbell told me how Snow Walker might dress, and she described his rattle. From my writing group, Margaretta Fleuter informed me of Aboriginal nuances she learned during her tenure teaching at Montreal Lake.

Also from my writing group, Sharon MacFarlane taught me pointed lessons on clarity and truth in the text. Lois Meaden and Ted Perrin told me of horses.

I thank Mavis and the children for putting up with my writing habits.

And above all, I thank my editors, Barbara Sapergia and Geoffrey Ursell. They were with the writing from the beginning. Like badgers they hung on, and like Pied Pipers they led me in new directions. I was privileged. To use Prairie parlance, they were there from the get-go.

ABOUT THE AUTHOR

LARRY WARWARUK is the author of the novels *The Ukrainian Wedding* and *Rope of Time,* and the non-fiction book *Red Finns of the Coteau.* His works have also been published in *Grain* and *NeWest Review* and broadcast on CBC Radio. He is a founder of the Snake Bite Players community theatre group in Beechy, Saskatchewan, and has received several Best Director awards in Saskatchewan Community Theatre competitions.

Born in Regina, Larry Warwaruk grew up in southern Saskatchewan, took education degrees at the University of Regina and the University of Oregon, and was a teacher and principal in central Saskatchewan for many years. He currently lives with his family in Outlook, Saskatchewan.

IN THE SAME BOAT

Celebrating Canadian Diversity

The Water *of* Possibility

by Hiromi Goto

Twelve-year-old Sayuri may be the only one who can save Living Earth from a terrible fate.

ISBN: 1-55050-183
6$9.95CN/$8.95US

Little Voice

by Ruby Slipperjack

An Ojibwa girl comes of age during a summer spent in the bush with her grand-mother.

ISBN: 1-55050-182-8
$9.95CN/$8.95US

Lost *in* Sierra

by Diana Vazquez

A young Canadian girl unravels a family mystery while visiting Spain.

ISBN: 1-55050-184-4
$8.95CN/$7.95US

Escape Plans

by Sherie Posesorski

Thirteen-year-old Becky confronts her fears at the height of the Cold War.

ISBN: 1-55050-177-1
$9.95CN/$8.95US

I Have Been *in* Danger

by Cheryl Foggo

Two young sisters grow closer together as one struggles to save the other.

ISBN: 1-55050-185-2
$8.95CN/$7.95US

Jason *and the* Wonder Horn

by Linda Hutsell-Manning

A magical horn trans-ports three kids back to medieval Germany.

ISBN: 1-55050-214-X
$9.95CN/$8.95US